DATE DUE

Demco No. 62-0549

WITHDRAWN

A BOAT
TO
NOWHERE

A BOAT TO NOWHERE

By
MAUREEN CRANE WARTSKI

Illustrated by
DICK TEICHER

THE WESTMINSTER PRESS
Philadelphia

BOOK DESIGN BY DOROTHY ALDEN SMITH

First edition

Published by The Westminster Press ®
Philadelphia, Pennsylvania

PRINTED IN THE UNITED STATES OF AMERICA

9 8 7 6 5 4 3 2 1

Library of Congress Cataloging in Publication Data

Wartski, Maureen Crane, 1940–
A boat to nowhere.

SUMMARY: Fleeing from agents of the new communist government in Vietnam, an old man and three children begin an endless and seemingly hopeless struggle for survival as boat people.
[1. Vietnam—Fiction. 2. Refugees—Fiction]
I. Teicher, Dick. II. Title.
PZ7.W2582Bo   [Fic]   79–28139
ISBN 0–664–32661–7

For Mike
and for Bert and Mark

I
MAI

1

"Loc!" Mai called. "Loc, where are you?"

Her little brother did not answer. Mai found herself trembling. The night was warm, but it was very dark. The tangle of bush and tall palm forest looked evil. Mai glanced over her shoulder, down the path that led to the Village. She could see no friendly lanterns. Almost everyone had gone to bed.

A snicker from somewhere in the brush caught Mai by surprise and scared her silly. Was Loc in there hiding?

"Loc," she said, her voice low, furious. "Come out right now or I will tell Grandfather. He thinks you're taking care of the water buffalo, and he sent me to help."

She waited for Loc to come out. There was no sound but the sigh of the wind and the whisper of the sea from the east.

"All right." Mai was disgusted. "I'm going to tell Grandfather you're playing games. I will tell Hong, too. It's dangerous this late at night. The whole forest is full of—"

Mai screamed. Something jumped out from the

black shadows and knocked her flat. Then Loc was on his knees beside her, pulling her to her feet.

"We have to get out of here!" he panted. "There's somebody out there! Somebody's in the forest!"

Mai's heart nearly stopped. "Loc, if you're trying to frighten me . . ." she threatened.

"I'm not! He's out there—a Monster Man! As big as Big Tam. He made horrible noises . . ." Loc dashed toward the Village, with Mai close behind. "If I'd stayed another second, he'd have eaten me!"

As they hurried by the first house, Big Tam's wife, Hong, stuck her head out of the door. *"Coi chung . . .* Be careful, you two!" she shouted. "What's the matter with you, running around at this time of night?"

"A monster in the forest!" Loc yelled. "A big hairy, hungry Monster Man—"

"Stop it!" Mai grabbed her little brother and shook him.

"Mai . . . Loc . . . are you all right?" Grandfather was hurrying out of their house. Big Tam brought a lantern, and the other villagers were gathering. "What's all this about a monster in the forest?" Grandfather demanded.

"I saw him!" Loc shrilled. "He put his hands on my shoulders . . ."

In the lantern light, Grandfather's face was stern. "Mai, did you see this Monster Man?" Mai shook her head. Her legs felt like rubber. Grandfather was taking Loc's crazy story seriously!

"Mai couldn't have seen him," Loc was crying. "I was hiding from her and I backed up and I stepped on this *foot . . .*" Loc's eyes were very round and scared. "It's true, Grandfather! It really happened!"

"We'll take a look." Grandfather straightened,

looked around at the villagers. "Tam, you and Duc come with me, please. The rest of you men can come if you like."

The other men quickly volunteered. Hong brought out another lantern and handed it to her brother-in-law, Duc the carpenter. "Do you want the women to come along too, *Thay* Van Chi?" she asked. The old man shook his head.

"No. Please stay with the children, Hong . . . all of you women and children stay here." Grandfather nodded to Big Tam and began to walk up the path to the forest.

Loc cried, "I should lead them! It's *my* monster!"

"Oh, no, you don't!" Hong grabbed Loc. "Didn't you hear Teacher Van Chi just now? You and your talk about monsters!"

Loc tried to wriggle loose, but Hong was very strong. Mai watched the lanterns disappearing into the darkness and drew closer to the big woman. The inky blackness of the night was menacing. Even the familiar Village with its wooden houses and thatch-palm roofs did not seem safe. In the east, the sea moaned.

"What do you think is out there, Hong?" Mai whispered.

Hong didn't answer, but there was murmured talk among the Village women.

"Probably nothing at all," Hong finally said.

"Maybe I was wrong," Loc said suddenly.

Hong gave him a shake. "I thought as much! Tell us what it was, eh? A banana tree? A shadow?"

"Maybe there were *two* Monster Men out there!" Loc cried.

The women's argument grew louder. One of them said, "Maybe it's over, then. They've found out about us. How could we hope to keep hidden forever? What will we do?"

"What are you talking about?" Mai asked.

Hong blew air through her fat cheeks and then said, "Nonsense! I don't believe a word of it. I'll tell you what we'll do. We'll follow the men and see what this 'Monster Man' is all about!"

Still holding on to Loc, Hong began to march along the path to the forest. Mai and the women followed. Soon they could see the ragged shadows of the trees that marked the edge of the forest. Mai was relieved to see her grandfather, and Duc. But where was Big Tam?

Suddenly Big Tam's voice yelled, "I have him!"

They could hear thrashing and crashing in the forest, a yell from big Tam. "Bite me, will you? You scorpion! Duc, help me . . ."

Duc jumped into the trees. Grandfather held his lantern high. Mai bit her knuckles and screamed. Even Hong gasped as something came hurtling out of the forest and landed on the ground before them all.

"There's your Monster Man!" Big Tam bellowed.

The dark shadow on the ground stirred, gathered itself into a squatting position. Dark eyes in a dirty face blinked warily in the light of the lantern.

"It's just a boy!" Hong muttered.

"Who are you?" Thay Van Chi demanded.

No answer. Big Tam aimed a cuff at the boy. "Answer Teacher Van Chi!" he roared.

The boy spat. Then, in an odd accent he muttered: *"Toi ten la Kien* . . . My name is Kien."

"How did you get here?" Big Tam demanded. "That's a city accent you talk with, boy." The boy shrugged rudely. The big man was about to cuff him again when the old man stopped him.

"My name is Kien"

"Don't hurt him, Tam." He looked at the boy and the boy stared back insolently. "Where do you come from, Kien?"

"Does it matter, Uncle? I lost my way. I suppose I took the wrong road. I was heading south—" He stopped and added in a beggar's whine, "Why did you jump at me and hurt me? I haven't done any harm!"

"No harm!" Hong let go of Loc and planted huge hands on her hips. "More than likely you were waiting for us to fall asleep so you could rob us."

Kien said, "I'm no thief, fat Auntie!"

Hong looked so indignant that the villagers began to laugh. Mai's grandfather did not laugh. "If you're not a thief, what do you do?" he asked.

"I work for my rice," Kien said. He began to scratch himself. "If you feed me, I'll do whatever you want me to do. I can fish, I can sail, I can plant rice, I can. . ."

"Keep away from that one, he's full of lice!" A Village woman snapped at her children. "I don't want him near you!"

Hong nodded, glaring at Kien.

"Don't let him into the Village, Thay Van Chi," her husband, Big Tam, urged. "If you do, he'll probably rob us. Besides . . ." He stopped, glanced at Mai and Loc, and seemed to force back words he wished to say. "Just give him some food and send him on his way."

Duc nodded. "He's come from the city. From *outside*," he said urgently.

Mai looked from Duc to Tam. Something was wrong. Why were the men so upset about this beggar boy? She looked closely at Kien. He was skinny and not much taller than she was. He looked to be a couple of years older than she. Grandfather had told her stories about beggars, but she had never seen one, for who needed to beg in the Village?

"I don't agree with you, Duc, Tam." Grandfather was saying. "I know what you are thinking, but this is only a child. He should have a bath and food and be welcome to stay with us as long as he wants."

"I'm no child. I'm fourteen!" Kien spat again, just missing Grandfather's foot. "I don't need your charity."

"Show respect!" Big Tam thundered, but the old man only looked at the boy.

"Can you walk?"

Kien shrugged.

"You can follow us back to the Village, then. You can stay with us if you care to."

Calling to his grandchildren, the old man began to walk back toward the Village. Kien remained sitting on the ground. In a little while, the other villagers followed Thay Van Chi, and Kien was left alone.

Mai thought that the strange beggar boy wasn't going to follow them. But when she peered over her shoulder, she saw that Kien had got to his feet and was slowly walking down the path to the Village.

2

Kien could certainly eat!

Mai watched amazed as the boy wolfed down four big bowls of rice and held out his bowl for more. Hong grumbled, but filled it up again. She said loudly that she was glad to cook and take care of Thay Van Chi and his family, but feeding a beggar brat she did not enjoy.

"If you're going to work for your rice as you boasted, you'll end up working for years!" she snapped in her loud voice.

Kien paid no attention. He slurped his rice, scooping it up into his mouth as if his chopsticks couldn't work fast enough. Mai couldn't help staring. Hadn't he ever learned any manners?

"What are you looking at?" Kien's narrow black eyes were unfriendly. "Haven't you ever seen a person eat?"

Mai blushed. "Grandfather wants to see you when you've eaten," she said. "He sent me to tell you."

"You'll have to wash first. No one is going to get near the teacher in your condition!" Hong insisted.

Kien gave a snort of laughter. "Too bad. I've grown fond of all my lice and fleas," he said.

He held out his rice bowl again, but Hong shook her head. "Your belly will explode if you eat more. Now, here is soap and a towel. Over there is the bathing area. There is a large jug of fresh water. Do you hear me? Now, wash!" Kien shrugged. "Here are some clean clothes. The clothes may not fit, but beggars can't choose. I am going to burn those rags you're wearing. Now, move!"

Kien grinned impudently. "Sure, fat one," he said, and sauntered off. Hong's face turned a brick red.

"Imagine having to cook for such a one at this time of night!" she grumbled. "Here, Mai. Help me clean up!"

While Mai helped Hong in the cooking area behind the house she could hear Duc and Big Tam talking with Grandfather. Mai caught the words "Kien" and "bad" and "he should go away."

"They don't want Kien to stay in the Village," Mai said to Hong. "Why?"

"He's a bad boy. Besides, he doesn't belong here."

"Loc and I weren't born in the Village," Mai pointed out. "Grandfather brought us here when Loc was just a baby. But *we* belong here!"

"That's different." Hong's face softened, and she turned to smooth back Mai's black hair. "From the time Tam and Duc found you in the forest, you and Loc have been like my own."

Mai nodded, remembering how kind this big, rough woman had been . . . how kind everyone else had been. The Village had taken them to their hearts, and soon Thay Van Chi had become the Village's revered teacher and its headman. Then why . . .

"Why doesn't anyone like Kien?" Mai wanted to know. "Is it because he's so rude?"

Hong's face softened, and she turned
to smooth back Mai's black hair

"That and other reasons."

What other reasons could there be? Mai wondered.

Hong began to busy herself stacking newly washed pots. Then she stopped to ask, "Mai, do you remember very much about your first home? In the city, I mean, when your parents still lived?"

Mai said, "I remember Mama and Father—a little. Mama was very pretty. She was always singing to me and playing with me. Father was a doctor. We had a big home with flowers in the garden. I was named for the flowers. . ."

"Do you remember why you left the city?" Hong asked.

"Father had to go away to be a doctor to the soldiers. He . . . he never came back." Even now the memory hurt Mai so much she hurried over this part. "Mama and I went to live with Grandfather in another city. Then Mama went to the hospital and Loc was born." Mai's voice dropped to a whisper. "Mama never came back from the hospital . . ."

"Ah," Hong said, her eyes full of tears.

"Grandfather said that the war had killed both Father and Mama. He took Loc and me away from the city. Loc was just a little baby and he cried a lot." Mai remembered that she had often cried herself as they walked hour after hour, from one town to another. Each time they arrived at a new village or town she had asked her grandfather whether they could stay there, but Thay Van Chi had kept on going. "It took us a long, long time to reach the Village," Mai told Hong. "I don't know how many towns and villages we stayed in . . . and we were often lost. One day we were so lost in the forest that I was sure we'd never find our way. Then Tam and Duc found us . . ."

There was a silence. Mai could hear Kien scrubbing himself some distance away in the bathing area. He sang as he sluiced water over himself:

"Oh, rifles are coming closer, my sister—
Ah, the cannon is booming, mother!
Why don't you take your baby and run away?"

"Stop that noise!" Hong shouted. Mai saw that the big woman was shaking, and suddenly she, too, was afraid. Why was Kien singing of rifles and cannon and running away? Why had Hong asked her to remember the old days?

"What has my remembering about the city to do with Kien not being welcome in the Village?" she asked.

Hong grunted. "You ask too many questions," she said in her normal voice. "Go away now. I'm too busy to talk to you."

Mai went around the corner of the house and saw Duc and Big Tam. Both men were just leaving after having talked with Grandfather. Neither Duc nor Big Tam looked happy, and Grandfather himself seemed thoughtful. Loc was sitting in the doorway half asleep.

"What is happening, Grandfather?" Mai asked, but the old man pretended not to hear her. Instead, he lifted Loc to his feet.

"Time for bed, my grandson," he said. "You've had a lot of excitement this evening. How will you get up for work and school tomorrow morning?"

Just then, Kien came around the corner of the house. Mai tried not to laugh. Kien was quite a sight! Hong had given him some of Big Tam's clothes, and they hung on Kien like great sacks. With his thin arms and legs, Kien looked like a spider.

"I'm tired, Uncle," Kien began. "I hope you won't want to talk too much."

"We'll sit outside—it's a fine, warm night," the old man replied. "Mai, you should go to bed with Loc. Morning comes early."

"But—!" Mai began to protest. Why should she and Loc be sent to bed like babies while Grandfather spoke to this stranger? Mai felt resentful, especially as Kien gave her a nasty smile. Loc started to argue too, but Grandfather just smiled and shook his head. Mai realized it was no use talking to him.

"Come on!" she snapped at Loc, and without another word pushed her complaining little brother inside the house.

The big one-room house served the family as eating, drinking, talking, and sleeping room. In the sputtering light of a lamp Mai moved past Grandfather's precious books, past the low wooden table surrounded by palm-leaf mats. In the corner farthest from the door she let down mosquito nets which were suspended from the ceiling and then spread sleeping mats on the wooden floor.

"Come on," she said to Loc, but Loc was still grumbling.

"I found that boy. Why should Grandfather send me to bed while he talks to Kien? Something strange is going on, Mai!"

Mai felt a shiver run up her backbone. Yes, she thought, something strange *is* going on. But what? She couldn't put her finger on what was bothering her, and it made her irritable. "It's time to go to bed," she told Loc. "If you hadn't been playing games so late at night, none of this would have happened!"

Loc stuck his tongue out at Mai. "You sound like Hong!" he said. "You're getting to look like her, too!"

At last, Loc settled down. Once he stretched out on his sleeping mat, his black eyes closed and he immediately fell asleep. Mai lay awake, eyes open in the warm darkness. She could hear a hum of voices from the outside, but she was too far from the doorway to make out what was being said. What *was* being said? What had frightened Hong and made Tam and Duc so nervous?

I have to know, Mai thought. She sat up, slipped

out from under the mosquito netting and tiptoed across the room. Stealthily, she hid behind the open door. Now she could hear Kien saying, "I'm surprised you didn't know any of this. Didn't you hear it on the radio?"

"We have no radios here," Grandfather replied. Peering through the doorway, Mai saw that he and Kien were squatting on the ground, facing each other.

"Didn't people from other villages tell you?" Kien sounded shocked.

"We are nowhere near another village. We are hidden away here."

Kien made a rude sound. "I'll say!" he muttered.

"You don't think much of our Village." The old teacher sounded amused. Kien shrugged. "Tell me . . . where did you live before you came here?"

"Many villages, many towns. I've lost count." Kien yawned, and added, "I always moved out when *they* came. They ruin everything."

Mai saw Grandfather's back stiffen, and again a sliver of fear crawled up her backbone. Who were "they"?

"Were any of them following you when you came this way?" Grandfather asked in a worried voice.

"No. Don't worry, Uncle. They couldn't find you, not easily, not with all this forest around you." The old man was silent and Kien added boastfully, "They almost got me once, you know. They came to a village where I was living for a while and said I was a bad influence on the village kids and they wanted to send me away for 'reeducation.' They'd have probably sent me to one of their new economic zones."

"What is that?" Grandfather asked. Again, Kien shrugged his bony shoulders.

"They have what they call resettlement camps. You're sent to hack out a new settlement in a jungle or forest. It's hard work, one of their ways of punishing people who don't agree with them."

There was a long silence, and Mai held her breath. Whoever "they" were, she didn't like them! She thought Grandfather would ask more about these dreadful people but he only said, "Will you stay with us for a time?"

"I don't know. As I said, I didn't intend to come this way at all. How do you people get around in this thick forest, anyway? Or don't you ever set foot out of this village?"

"There are certain trails in the forest. If you stay with us, you will learn of them. But don't you have any family, Kien? Friends?"

It seemed to Mai that the strange boy hesitated before saying, "No one. I like being on my own. Now, Uncle, I'm tired of your questions. Either throw me out of your village or let me sleep somewhere."

"Big Tam and Hong have agreed to let you stay with them for the time being," the old man said. "However, I must ask you, Kien, not to repeat anything about . . . about what is going on outside the Village. I don't want you to say anything that might frighten the children."

Kien stood up. "That's fine with me," he said.

As Kien began to walk away from the old man, Mai watched Big Tam step out from his house to show the boy where he could rest for the night. Thay Van Chi watched Kien go, too. "Soon." Mai heard him sigh. "Soon, now . . ."

Soon . . . what? Mai began to tremble, just as Hong had trembled earlier in the evening. Something was going to happen. What it was Mai could not guess, but there was a tightness in her chest that reminded her of being lost and afraid in the dark. Something was going to happen and even Grandfather could not stop it.

She slipped back to her sleeping mat and lay down beside Loc. She cuddled up against her little brother, whispering, "I'm afraid . . . I'm so afraid. Oh, why did he have to come?"

Somehow, Kien's coming had changed the Village. From now on, life in the Village would never be quite the same . . .

3

Mai woke up late the next morning. Usually she opened her eyes around dawn, dressed, and helped Hong with the morning meal. That morning, the sun had already risen and Loc was gone. She could hear Hong scolding loudly outside the house.

"For shame! You want more food, do you? Is your stomach a bottomless well? *Thoi-dii . . .* enough! Thay Van Chi doesn't have to feed you a bushel of good rice, worthless one!" Still complaining, she lumbered through the doorway of the house to place a tray of food on the table before Mai's grandfather.

"Good morning, Hong." Grandfather's voice had a smile in it. "I see the boy is still here."

"It's too bad he didn't run away during the night!" Hong snapped.

The old man laughed. Mai saw that his sleeping mat had been neatly folded and he was dressed for work. Grandfather was the Headman and also the Teacher. By rights he should not have had to work at all. However, he probably worked harder than anyone else in the Village. He helped the women with the vegetable patch, or gave Duc a hand carpentering, or went with Big Tam to fish in the Village's one boat, the *Sea Breeze*.

"Thay Van Chi," Hong said, "you can laugh, but I am serious. That's a bad boy, and I don't like him living here."

"Is he bad because he has no parents?" The old man's voice was stern. "Because he had to live by his wits?"

"It's not that. Last night, after he came to our house, he told us things about the . . . the war. He enjoyed frightening us!"

Mai felt last night's fear rise up in her so strongly that she nearly cried out. She lay very still as the old man turned to look at her. "Hush! Speak softly, Hong. Mai might hear you . . ."

Hong said in a low voice, "Some of the things he told us . . . Why, I had nightmares! And the life he's led! His parents died when he was a baby and he had to live with relatives, who abandoned him when they ran out of money. He grew up in an orphanage, hating it. Then he took money from the orphanage and ran away! He's been living on his own since he was about eight—nearly half his life!" She shook her head. "It's left him hard, Thay Van Chi. It's taken all the goodness out of him."

The old man was grave. "He spoke about these things to me last night, but I'll have another talk with him. He mustn't tell the children anything about the war."

"Tam warned him about that—"

Before Hong could go on, Loc bounced into the house asking, "Mai, are you asleep?"

"Who could sleep when you make all that noise?" Mai was disgusted with Loc. If he hadn't come in, she

Grandfather was the Headman
and also the Teacher

might have learned more about Kien . . . and the war.
Was the war coming closer? Mai asked herself. Though
war was going on in Vietnam, Grandfather never spoke
of it. In the Village, Mai had even forgotten about the
war that had killed her parents. Forgotten, that is, until
Kien arrived last night. Again she thought, Why did he
have to come here?

"Are you going to lie there all day, Miss Lazy?" Hong demanded, fists on her big hips.

Mai hurried through her morning duties, tidying up the sleeping mats and mosquito nets. Then she hurried outside to the bathing area and washed, readying herself for the new day. By the time she joined Grandfather and Loc at breakfast, they had finished eating. Loc was telling Grandfather about the clever magic tricks Kien could perform.

"He took a pebble and made it disappear," Loc said, "and he can sing funny songs! Oh, there he is. Kien, sing Grandfather a song!"

Kien, grinning, was lounging against the open door. He was wearing Big Tam's undershirt over a pair of ragged shorts.

"Good morning, little brother," he said to Loc. "I can't sing today. I have to work for my rice."

"The question is, what will you do?" Grandfather smiled.

"I can do anything." Kien came inside the house, squatting between Loc and Grandfather. "I took a walk down to the lagoon this morning," he went on. "I saw a boat moored there. It was a small boat . . . just a common fishing boat, but I could sail it. I'm a good sailor, you know. And I am a good fisherman."

"That is Big Tam's boat, the *Sea Breeze*, and I wouldn't let him overhear that you think it is small," Grandfather said, amused. "He is our fisherman, and a small village like this one needs only one fisherman."

"I could help Big Tam," Kien pointed out.

"Big Tam would never let you into that boat," Mai cut in. "He never lets anyone into the *Sea Breeze*, except Grandfather."

"Besides, Big Tam has gone out to sea," Grandfather added. "Fishermen get up early. Kien, you can help the women with the vegetables today."

Kien made a face. "I hate weeding and hoeing," he said. He added mockingly, "I suppose it is a small vegetable patch, like this small village of only six families!"

"We like it here," Mai snapped. She hoped this would embarrass Kien. It didn't.

"We may be small but we all work hard," the old man said gently. "Big Tam is our fisherman, and he supplies us with all the fresh fish we can eat. His brother, Duc, is our carpenter. It was Duc who built the *Sea Breeze* with his own hands. The rest of us help the women in the vegetable patch or help Duc in his repair work."

"I'd like to go fishing with Big Tam," Kien said. "I'm the best fisherman there is. I used to sail a big boat for a fisherman in another village."

"Let's stick to vegetables today." Grandfather got up. "Today I'm helping Duc and the other men make repairs around the Village, so I must be going. Mai will show you where to get hoes and a basket, Kien. Enjoy your morning."

Kien hardly waited for the old man to walk out of earshot before groaning, "Just my luck. I had to get stuck in a miserable, flea-bitten little village!"

Mai's cheeks grew hot. Without a word she heaped breakfast things pell-mell onto a tray and carried them out into the back for Hong. If Kien despises us, why does he stay here? She wondered. And then came another thought: Does he *want* something from us?

From the cooking area she could hear Loc speaking to Kien. "You'll like the Village when you get used to it, Kien. It's pretty. See? The forest is all around us.

Grandfather says that we have no neighbors except for the trees, the sea, and the sky."

"What a bore!" Kien mocked. Then he added, as if to himself, "But you *are* really hidden here. I wouldn't have found you myself except that I lost my way. No wonder nobody bothered you here!"

Who would *want* to bother us? Mai wondered. Kien knew something she didn't. She wished . . .

"Kien! Loc!" Hong's loud voice interrupted her thoughts. "What are you dawdling around for? Get going! Loc, you get out there and take the buffalo to pasture. Mai, where are you? Show this good-for-nothing where to get his hoe and basket!"

Loc hurried off at once. He enjoyed his morning's work. Taking care of the Village's big gray water buffalo which gave milk and helped thresh rice at harvesttime was good fun. He and a few of his friends would spend all day letting the buffalo graze and bathe in the marsh near the vegetable patch.

"See you!" Loc called to Mai. "See you in school, Mai!"

"School?" Kien asked, following Mai to pick up a hoe and a basket at the back of the house.

"Yes. Grandfather teaches everyone in the afternoon, even the adults," Mai explained.

"So that's why they call the old one '*Thay*' . . . 'Teacher' Van Chi." Kien didn't sound impressed. "School's a waste of time. I went once, that was enough!"

"Where did you go to school?" Mai asked, curious.

"In Saigon." Kien flipped his hoe in the air, caught it, grinned at Mai. "Bet you don't even know where that is."

"As it happens, I do!" Kien needed to be taught a

lesson, and no mistake! "Grandfather teaches us geography. We know all there is to know about the country . . ."

Kien burst out laughing. "You know all there is to know about—that's good. Oh, that's good!" Still hooting, he walked off, leaving Mai fuming. Kien was rude and he was insulting and she couldn't stand him. Nor did she trust him!

Mai took her temper out on the weeds that needed to be pulled from the vegetable patch. Not that anybody really worked very hard. What weeding and watering needed to be done was done at a leisurely pace, and there was a lot of laughter. The women joked and gossiped and watched the small children, who played with mud pies by the side of the patch or plaited flowers into chains. Mai took care not to get anywhere close to Kien, but she had to admit that he worked harder than all the rest of them put together. Once started, he weeded, watered, and straightened rows without dawdling or complaining. Mai was impressed that such a skinny boy could carry heavy buckets of water and work so tirelessly.

After several hours, Hong halted the work. "It's time to rest," she called. The women wiped their foreheads, rested their hoes, and brought out packets of cold rice, wrapped in cool banana leaves, and fruit. Hong had packets for Mai, Loc, and today, for Kien also.

Mai was hungry. As soon as she had her food she started to walk away from the field. She had not walked far, however, before she hesitated and looked back at Kien, who had squatted down alone some distance from the others. Oh, well, she thought. I'll try to be friendly one more time.

31

"Would you like to come and eat your lunch with Loc and me?" she asked Kien. "I'll show you a pretty place to eat, if you like."

Kien shrugged. "Why not?" he asked.

Mai began to lead up the path to the marshy area beyond the field. Here, the buffalo was at pasture. Loc and his friends were having a fine time, and Mai could hear shrieks of laughter as she and Kien drew closer.

"Hello, Mai!" Loc called, as soon as the two came into view. "Did you bring food? I'm starving!"

Mai gave Loc his lunch and showed Kien where she generally sat—a flat, gray stone near the marsh under a sweeping trail of bougainvillea flowers. It was a gravestone. As in most Vietnamese villages, ancestors were buried near the rice paddies. This allowed their souls to grow into rice, which would nourish the living.

"Here is where we plant our rice in the monsoon season," Mai explained to Kien, who sat quietly munching his food. "In a couple of months, when the monsoon rains start, our village is really going to be busy."

Kien grunted. "You call this a village? Six families and an old goat for a headman . . ."

Before he could go on, Mai reached over and pushed him hard, knocking him off the gray stone.

"You take that back!" she shouted. "Don't you dare talk about Grandfather or our village that way!"

Kien laughed, picked himself up, and went on eating. "Your precious village is a poor place," he mocked.

Mai was too furious to reply. Instead, she got up and went over to where Loc and his friends were sliding up and down the water buffalo's back. Sometimes they landed full tilt in the squishy mud, and Loc was covered with it.

"Can't you even wash your hands before you eat?" Mai scolded, for Loc was eating as he played.

Loc stuck his tongue out at Mai and popped rice into his mouth. Kien snickered. "You should hear yourself! You sound like a regular little mother!"

Mai had had enough of Kien for one day. "What do you know about mothers? I'll bet you don't even remember your own!"

Kien shrugged. "I don't need one. I've looked after myself pretty well."

"Really? Is that why you went to an orphanage? If you looked after yourself so well, why would anyone put you in an orphanage?"

"I was really young, then. I left soon enough."

"They probably asked you to leave!" Mai exclaimed. "I'll bet they didn't want you around!"

For the first time, she saw that she had hurt him. A slow flush stained Kien's sunburned cheeks, and Mai was sorry. She started to tell Kien this, but before she could speak Kien mumbled, "I wasn't thrown out. I left because of Jim."

"Jim? What a strange name!" Mai said. "Who is Jim?"

Kien hesitated, and then put his hand into the pocket of his shorts. When he pulled his hand out, something glittered. Mai gasped.

"It's a wristwatch . . . gold," Kien said proudly. "Jim gave this to me. He was my friend."

"I thought you told Grandfather you didn't have any friends," Mai murmured, looking at the gleaming wristwatch. The thought flashed into her mind that Kien must have stolen the watch, but she pushed it away, ashamed. Perhaps this boy wasn't so bad after all. Perhaps it just took him time to make friends. "It's beautiful," Mai said. "Grandfather has a watch, but nothing like this."

"You can touch it if you like," Kien said, pleased and proud. "Jim was an American, see. He came to Vietnam to fight. He flew a plane. One day he said he'd take me back to America on that plane."

"Then why didn't he?" Mai asked.

"Because I didn't want to go." Kien put the watch back into his pocket. "Nobody ever makes me do something I don't want to do."

"But you said he was your friend, so why—"

"What do you know, anyway?" Kien snorted. "You're just a country dummy. Buried in this rotten, stinking little village . . ."

Mai, hurt, snapped right back, "I don't believe a word about your 'friend' Jim! I bet you stole the watch! When we get back to the Village, I'm going to tell Hong that—"

Before she could go on, Kien reached out and grasped her wrists. "If you tell anyone about this watch, I'll make you sorry!" he snarled.

Mai stared at him, shocked. He was hurting her wrists and the look in his eyes scared her. Just then, they heard a bell being rung back at the Village.

"Hey, Mai . . . school!" Loc cried, sliding down the patient buffalo's back one last time. "Let's take the buffalo back to the Village!"

Kien gave Mai's wrists a shake. "Tell me you promise, or you'll be sorry!" he repeated.

Mai hesitated, too proud to back down. What would Kien do if she didn't promise? She looked into his narrow, angry eyes and knew he'd think of something mean!

"All right!" She cried. "But I think you're horrible!

I wish you'd go away and never come back here again. Who'd want to be your friend?"

Kien dropped her wrists and turned away. "Who cares what you think?" he snarled.

Mai ran past the boy and followed Loc and the other little boys who were riding the water buffalo back to the Village. Loc was filthy with mud, and in a way Mai was glad. She would now have to get busy and clean Loc off, which meant she didn't have time to think of Kien. Nevertheless, she did think of him. She didn't understand him. And she certainly didn't like him. "I wish he'd go away," Mai muttered to herself.

It was time for school. There was no schoolhouse in the Village so Grandfather usually taught outside, in front of his house. By the time Mai joined the others, the villagers had formed a large semicircle around the old man. All the children were grouped in front of Thay Van Chi, and most of the adults squatted behind the children. The only ones missing were Big Tam, who was probably still out fishing, and Hong. Kien, Mai noted, was missing too.

She slipped in among the children as Grandfather asked, "Now, who can tell me how many years we lived under Chinese rule?"

Loc was good at history. His hand shot up at once. "That was a long, long time ago, Grandfather," he began importantly. "We were called Nam Viet, then. In those ancient times, the Chinese conquered us and ruled us for a thousand years."

Grandfather smiled pleasedly at Loc. "A thousand years *is* a long time," he said. "Eventually our people became free, isn't that so?"

"Tell me, Thay Van Chi," Duc said, "why is it that people have always wanted to conquer us? The Chinese first, and then the French . . ." He scratched his head in a puzzled way. "I can't make it out."

"Oh, I know that, *Bác* Duc," Mai said. "It's because we are a beautiful country." Everyone applauded, laughing. "Isn't that so, Grandfather?"

"You are right," her grandfather said, and the laughter stopped suddenly. "Our country is the most beautiful country in the world . . . to us. It was so, and it is so, and will always be." Mai saw Duc look away, coughing and wiping his eyes. Why, she thought, Uncle Duc is crying. But why? "When I was young," Grandfather went on, "I traveled all over the world. I had adventures sailing the South China Sea in a boat not much bigger than the *Sea Breeze*. I have visited Malaysia, Thailand . . . even America! But though each of these countries was new and exciting, none of them was as beautiful as our country."

Mai felt a thrill of happiness as she listened to Grandfather. She could tell how dearly he loved Vietnam when he talked like this, and besides, he told such wonderful stories. Sometimes he told fables, like the one about an ugly toad who went all the way to Heaven to ask for rain during a drought. Sometimes he told stories about ancient heroes of Vietnam. The ones Mai liked best were the stories Grandfather told about his own adventures.

Apparently everyone else thought so too, because one of the children cried, "Please, Thay Van Chi, tell us a story!"

"What?" the old teacher cried, pretending to be horrified. "What about our history lesson?"

"We will study later! You tell stories so well," one of Loc's friends begged.

"Very well, but be attentive!" Thay Van Chi said,

and everyone drew nearer. Mai heard a soft movement somewhere behind her. Turning, she saw that Kien had drifted over and was leaning against the wall of Grandfather's house. He made a face at her and she quickly turned her back on him. She just wasn't going to let Kien spoil the story for her!

"Here is the story," Thay Van Chi was saying. "Once, when I was a young man of about nineteen, I was very restless. My parents had plenty of money, and they spoiled me. Everything I wanted, I had, even to a good education. Well, my father became sick of my restlessness and sent me to sea with an old friend of his who owned a small shipping line. Work on board one of his friend's ships would be good for me, my father said."

He paused, adding, "During my first voyage on the ship, a terrible storm came up. The ship wasn't a big one, nor a very strong one. I was terrified that we were going to be wrecked. Fortunately, Heaven was kind to us and we were able to get home in safety. Do you know the first thing I did when I got my feet on good Vietnamese soil? I kneeled down and kissed the ground because I had never seen such beautiful land."

"Old man, you lie!"

Everyone turned. Kien had risen to his feet and was sneering at Thay Van Chi. "Why don't you tell them the truth about the 'beautiful land'?" He shouted. "This beautiful country you talk about doesn't exist anymore!"

Thay Van Chi was very pale. "Show some respect!" he said angrily, and Duc bounced to his feet.

"Thay Van Chi, please let me throw this beggar out of the Village!" he pleaded. "He's bad . . . through and through!"

Kien made a rude noise and walked away. "You'd better stop living in your dreamworld, Uncle," he said over his shoulder.

No one spoke for a moment, then a woman snapped, "I'm with Duc. We should throw that bad one out of the Village."

Mai found herself nodding. Yes, Kien was a bad one. Insulting the Village, insulting Grandfather, lying about the country. What does he want from us? she wanted to shout.

"*Cho*... wait," the old man said quickly, as several villagers got to their feet. "The boy knows no better. Perhaps, since he doesn't care for our village, he will leave us. Now, who knows the principal rivers of our country?"

They were still talking about rivers when a loud voice interrupted them. Hong was running up the path, her face red and agitated.

"Thay Van Chi!" she was shouting. "You must come and help Tam! He has cut himself badly with Duc's ax," and the big woman burst into sobs.

4

When they had calmed Hong down, she told them, between sobs, that Tam had gone into the forest to look for a piece of wood.

"He wanted to repair the *Sea Breeze,*" Hong wailed. "He went to your house, Duc, but you weren't there. Tam just took your ax and went into the forest. He started to cut. The ax slipped and caught him in the leg . . ."

"Where is he?" Duc was ghost-pale.

"In the forest," Hong sobbed. Mai's grandfather turned to her.

"Mai, get my black bag with the medicines. Follow after us. Hong, show us where Tam is!"

Mai raced into the house. The black bag with Grandfather's precious supply of disinfectant, pills, and bandages was right next to his books. It took her only seconds to snatch up the bag, but the villagers were already at the outskirts of the forest when she caught up with them.

"He should have called me! A fisherman can't work with wood!" Duc was saying. "Hong, thank heaven you found Tam . . ."

"It wasn't I who found him, Duc. It was that beggar brat, that Kien." Hong turned to Grandfather. "Thay Van Chi, it's really bad . . ." and she began to cry again.

It took some time to reach Big Tam. He was pale and was lying very still under a tall tree. The small ax was flung to one side. Kien was kneeling beside Big Tam. As the villagers hurried up, they saw that Kien was doing something to the big man's leg.

"Get away from my brother!" Duc shouted.

Kien didn't answer. Mai saw that he had tied a piece of rope directly above a horrible cut on Big Tam's leg. As they watched, Kien pushed a sturdy twig under the rope, next to Big Tam's skin, and began to twist it in a corkscrew motion. The rope tightened, and Big Tam groaned.

"Get away!" Duc said again, but the old man stopped him.

"Where did you learn to tie a tourniquet?" he asked Kien, as he squatted down beside the boy. "It was clever of you to think of it. The big fellow could have bled to death."

"I don't know what it's called. I saw a doctor do this to someone in the city," Kien mumbled.

Mai watched, silent as the others, as the old man began to examine Tam's wound. Big Tam opened his eyes and whispered, "Am I going to die, Thay Van Chi?"

At this, Hong burst into wails, and Duc tried to comfort her. "Hush, woman! Of course he's not going to die! Thay Van Chi's here, isn't he?" But Duc himself was white and shaking all over.

Mai couldn't blame him. She felt sick herself, and when she glanced at Loc she saw that her brother looked ill, too. Grandfather was saying, "Of course you're not going to die. You're as tough as our water buffalo. But this is a nasty cut, I am going to have to clean it and stitch the skin together. We must get you back to the Village."

The men volunteered to carry Big Tam, and Grandfather sent the women ahead to boil water. Mai went with them. Hong was too upset to take charge, so she helped put large pots of water on the fires to heat, and by the time the men arrived, the water had begun to steam.

Kien accompanied the men who were carrying Big Tam into Tam's house. After a moment, Kien came hurrying out.

"The old man wants water," he shouted at Mai, who ignored him. "Didn't you hear?" Kien yelled even louder. He came racing over to where Mai stood beside a pot of near-boiling water. "Hurry up . . . I'm supposed to bring that hot water to him right away," Kien continued importantly.

"You?" Mai asked, surprised. Kien grinned mockingly.

"Me. I know what I'm doing, little sister."

"I am *not* your little sister!" Mai snapped. Then she was ashamed of herself. Grandfather was trying to help Tam . . . and so was Kien. "Do whatever you want," she said to Kien. "This water is nearly ready."

Kien poked his nose close to the water and nodded with a superior air that made Mai want to smack him. Then he said, "It'll do, I suppose," and began to haul the pot off to Big Tam's house. Grandfather appeared in the doorway.

"Kien . . . hurry! I need you to help me," he ordered.

Kien . . . to help? Mai felt something twist inside her. Then, again she was ashamed. If anyone could help Big Tam, she was glad. Only . . . only why did it have to be Kien?

The afternoon wore on slowly. For over an hour, Grandfather did not come out of Big Tam's house. Hong, Duc, and Kien remained with him. The other villagers milled around, discussing Big Tam's accident and how Kien had found him.

"Heaven must have sent him to help Tam," the villagers said to one another. No one seemed to remember that they had all been ready to throw Kien out of the Village before Big Tam's accident.

Finally Hong came out of her house. She looked pale, but she was smiling, and she hugged Loc and Mai.

"Tam is going to be all right," she said. The villagers clapped their hands together and began to talk very loudly.

"You see? Heaven *did* send that boy to us! If he hadn't been there . . ."

"You heard Thay Van Chi! If that boy hadn't twisted that rope around Big Tam's leg . . ."

Hong raised her loud voice above the noise. "Thay Van Chi has cleaned the wound and stitched it, and now it is up to Heaven to heal Tam," she announced. "But I am thankful." There were tears in her eyes.

"Where is Grandfather?" Loc wanted to know.

"With Tam. He's going to stay with Tam for a while. I have to help too. Mai, you cook the rice for the family this evening. The other women will help you."

So Mai was kept busy cooking, and the other children ran back and forth from Big Tam's house, peeping in and reporting how the big man looked.

"He's smiling, so he must be feeling better," Loc

told Mai sometime later as she lifted the cover of a pot and checked to see whether the rice was ready. "I'm hungry, Mai! So is Grandfather, and Kien, too!"

"Kien?" Mai asked, and Loc nodded.

"Grandfather says you're to bring rice for Kien and for him to Tam's house," he announced importantly. "Kien's helping Grandfather."

So Kien had been promoted to Grandfather's special assistant! She didn't mind it, not really, and she did take rice in big bowls to Grandfather and to Loc and even to Kien. But when Kien gave her his nasty smile and took the rice bowl from her, she burst out, "What makes you so important all of a sudden?"

"Mai," Grandfather pointed out, "Kien helped me all afternoon!"

"Why couldn't Loc or I have helped you?"

Grandfather must have been very tired, for he snapped, *"Thoi-dii . . .* that's enough! Kien knew what he was doing. He helped me. He worked like a grown man today."

Like a . . . Mai looked at Kien, who was eating his rice in pretended modesty. "This is good rice, little sister," he said in a mock-polite voice. Mai stamped out of Tam's house in a huff. But she heard Kien say, "She doesn't like me. I don't know why. I never bothered her or did anything . . ."

Oh, that Kien! It didn't help Mai's temper when she overheard some of the village women telling Hong: "The old saying is true. If you do a good deed, Heaven rewards you. You and your husband took in that boy, and now that boy rewards you!"

Mai wondered if Hong was going to stand still and listen to this nonsense, but Hong just nodded. "I know. He worked very hard to help Thay Van Chi today. It makes me ashamed for the way I have spoken about that boy. Now I know he acts in that rude manner, sometimes, because he doesn't know any better. He has a good heart, that much is sure!"

Mai's self-control just about snapped. She wanted to shout, He's not good . . . not at all! If she had, the villagers would not have believed her. Right then they thought Kien was wonderful!

The feeling grew stronger as the days passed. All of a sudden Kien became an important person in the Village. Women cooked special dishes for him. Big Tam praised Kien to the skies. The Village children began to follow Kien about, as if he were one of those heroes Grandfather told stories about.

It made Mai sick. It made her even angrier when Kien pretended to change, to become friendly and anxious to please. He worked hard at any task set for him, ran errands for the women, visited Big Tam. Only to Mai was he the mocking, rude Kien who had first come to the Village. When he was alone with Mai, Kien would still make fun of the Village until she itched to slap him. She knew that Kien had not changed at all, and she wished that he would leave.

Kien didn't leave. What happened next seemed horrible to Mai. Kien got his wish about sailing Big Tam's precious boat, the *Sea Breeze*! Mai couldn't believe it when her grandfather announced one evening that Big Tam had decided to let Kien sail the *Sea Breeze* until he had recovered from his wound.

"Big Tam doesn't let anyone use the boat," Mai protested. "He never let Loc or me near the boat . . ."

"Loc's too young, and you're a girl," Grandfather pointed out. "Big Tam thinks only boys should be allowed to fish."

"But Kien doesn't really know how to sail! I'll bet he wrecks the *Sea Breeze*."

"Don't worry. Kien won't go out alone in the *Sea Breeze* . . . not at first, anyhow. I will go with him and teach him."

"You!" Mai was beyond words. She had often asked Grandfather to teach her how to sail the *Sea Breeze*, but he had always put her off. And now he was going to teach Kien! Hot jealousy and hurt clogged her throat so that she couldn't speak.

"Kien says he is used to boats. If this is true, it will help the Village. None of us are good fishermen except for Big Tam, and not many of us can sail the boat. Besides, Kien saved—"

"I know! I've heard it often enough! He saved Big Tam's life!" Mai snapped, and when her grandfather told her to have more respect, she ran out of the house with the tears hot and gritty under her eyelids. Kien on the *Sea Breeze*! It was too much to take.

Naturally, Kien rubbed her nose in it too. "You heard that I'm the new captain of the *Sea Breeze*," he told her later that day. "I'll take you and Loc sailing someday."

"Will you?" Loc was delighted. He liked Kien, who made him laugh with his magic tricks and who sang so many interesting songs. "When can we go?"

Mai said, "Who is 'we'? I wouldn't sail with Kien. He'd drown us both!"

Kien laughed softly. "Jealous?" he crooned, and Mai could have thrown something at him. Oh, yes! She could have picked up a rock and thrown it right at his ugly head.

After that, Mai avoided Kien, or tried to. It wasn't easy to avoid anyone in a place as small as the Village.

And then, people just naturally talked about Kien. Whenever she visited Big Tam, the big man would tell Mai about how well Kien was doing, sailing the *Sea Breeze*. "Thay Van Chi says that he's a natural sailor, that boy," he would say. "As soon as my leg heals, I may even make him my assistant."

"But why Kien?" Mai burst out, and the big man looked at her in surprise.

"Why," he said, "he's the oldest boy in the Village, after all"—as if Kien had been in the Village all his life!

But none of this hurt as much as Loc's admiration for the nasty boy. Loc could suddenly talk about no one but Kien, Kien, Kien. One day, soon after Mai's talk with Big Tam, Loc showed her a wooden boat Kien had skillfully whittled out of one of Duc's wood scraps.

"Kien made it for me," Loc said proudly.

"It's a stupid boat," Mai said. "Duc could have made you a much nicer boat if you'd asked him."

"I like it . . . it's my boat." Loc looked hurt. "What's the matter with you, anyway? I think Kien is nice. All my friends think so, too. Everyone does, except you!"

"I don't want to talk about it," Mai said stiffly.

"You always get angry when anyone talks about Kien," Loc continued. "Kien says that's because you're jealous."

Mai yelled, "Just leave me alone! Who asked you to discuss me with Kien? Who asked you to come and bother me? Now go away!"

Loc went, but he didn't stop talking about Kien.

Days slid into weeks. Big Tam's leg healed slowly, and everyone knew he was itching to be back sailing the *Sea Breeze*. But under Thay Van Chi's orders, he limped around at home, playing with the children, helping Duc whenever he could. Kien continued to sail the *Sea Breeze,* and even Mai had to admit he brought in lots of fish. Often Grandfather would let Kien take the boat out into the lagoon himself, and Kien would come home in the evening, swaggering like a grown man, demanding food. Hong always had good food waiting for Kien, saying he was too skinny.

One day Mai burst out, "He's not skinny anymore! He's as fat as a pig!"

The boy had lost his bony look. His stomach no longer caved inward, and because the Village women had sewed some clothes for him that fit, he no longer flapped around comically in Big Tam's castoffs. His flesh had filled out, and he had grown a few inches. He didn't look like a spider anymore.

"If you don't stop feeding him, he'll explode," Mai told Hong.

Hong laughed. "Feeding the hungry is a good deed," she said.

"You didn't say that when Kien first came!" Mai shouted and went away, leaving Hong to stare after her thoughtfully. When her temper cooled, Mai felt sorry. She was shouting at everyone lately, but it wasn't really her fault. Couldn't people see through Kien? Couldn't they see that he was just as sneery and rude and mean as ever?

That same evening, Kien came to see them. Mai, Loc, and Grandfather were sitting in front of their house, watching the sky turn from blue to purple, when Kien walked over and squatted down beside Grandfather.

"Hello," he said. "I've come to ask you a question, Uncle."

Hong laughed.
"Feeding the hungry is a good deed."

"And what is that?" Grandfather smiled, while Mai bristled.

"Do you think it'll be a fine day tomorrow?" Kien asked. He rubbed his nose with the back of his hand. "Do you think it would be a fine day to take Loc and Mai for a ride on the *Sea Breeze*?"

"A ride on the *Sea Breeze*?" Loc nearly knocked Mai sideways as he jumped all over Kien. "Really? Grandfather, can we go?"

"*You* can," Mai snapped. "I'm not interested!"

There was a little silence. "If you don't go, Loc cannot go either," Grandfather said. "Someone must be with Loc. Kien will have to do the fishing and can't take care of him."

"That's sense," Kien agreed.

"Then get someone else to watch Loc!" Mai said. She started to get to her feet, but Grandfather suddenly reached out and touched her cheek very gently.

"Of course, it is up to you. But you always said that you wanted to sail on the *Sea Breeze.*"

"Yes, but—" But not with Kien, Mai thought. Before she could refuse again, Loc began to plead.

"Mai, can't we go? I'll be good. I'll be so good! Mai, it'll feel so nice to be on the sea. We can fish and swim, and Hong will make us good food to take . . ." He was almost in tears.

"Well?" Grandfather asked Mai, and Mai knew that if she refused, she would appear mean and unkind.

"Oh, all right," she muttered. Loc whooped with joy, and Grandfather smiled.

Kien looked pleased, too. "Be ready tomorrow early," was all he said, but Mai puzzled about the expression in his eyes. Why should Kien be pleased that she was going along? Was he planning some kind of trick? She decided to be on her guard all the time they were out on the lagoon.

Even so, Mai's heart leaped the next morning when she and Loc walked down to the cove where the *Sea Breeze* was moored. Beyond the boat lay the lagoon, a soft gray stained by a red sunrise. Kien was already checking the fishing net and the *Sea Breeze*'s sail, while Big Tam hobbled about on the beach, waving the crutch Duc had made for him as he gave Kien instructions.

"Stay close to the shore today," Big Tam was saying as Mai and Loc came up. "I'm not fond of the way the sky looks. Red sunrise . . . That might mean storm. Remember, we're getting closer to the monsoon season, and at this time of year the weather can change suddenly." He gave Mai and Loc a big grin. "Ready to set sail with Captain Kien, are you?"

Loc gave a squeal of joy, and Kien said bossily, "Mai, Loc, help me with the fishing net. We'd better get going. We're late as it is."

For two piasters, Mai thought, she would leave "Captain" Kien and Loc standing there and run back to

Kien was already checking the fishing net and the Sea Breeze's sail

the Village. Instead, she found herself sitting in the stern of the *Sea Breeze* with Loc while Kien pushed the boat out into the water. Then they were waving at Big Tam and sailing into the reddish dawn.

Well, she was here now, so she might as well try to enjoy the day. Mai closed her eyes and rubbed her hands over the sides of the *Sea Breeze*. She wished that she and Loc were alone on the old boat, so that she could truly enjoy its smells and feel. She felt its age in the smooth wood, loved the smells of wood and tar and fish.

"It's a lovely boat," Kien said. She opened her eyes quickly, ready for some new mockery or rudeness, and heard Kien say, "When I was a kid—really little, I mean —my father had a boat like this one. It reminded me of that old boat right away."

Mai opened her mouth to say something, but nothing came out. Kien meant what he was saying! His cheeks flushed a little as he ran his hand up and down the side of the boat. "The wood speaks to you," he said softly.

Loc was still waving to Big Tam, shouting boast-fully that they would bring back enough fish to bury the Village. Mai looked at Kien and thought of what Hong had said long ago, that Kien had had to work his way through life without anyone to help him. She had memories of her mother and father, and there had al-ways been Grandfather and Hong to care for her.

Maybe he just doesn't know how to be nice, she thought, and as she thought, Kien said offhandedly, "I suppose it sounds crazy to you, but sailing along in the *Sea Breeze* these last few days I've been remembering about the time I was a little kid." He shrugged. "Does-n't make sense, does it?"

"Yes, it does," she said, and before she could think, she smiled at Kien. "I understand," she said. "Really."

"You're a smart girl," Kien said, with his old impudent grin. But somehow it didn't bother her. Behind that grin Mai could sense the fact that Kien wanted to be friends. It seemed as if a dark cloud had lifted from over the *Sea Breeze,* and Mai was suddenly happy.

"Well, Captain," she demanded, "what are we waiting for? The fish are out there, ready for us!"

They sailed before a fair wind until they were well away from shore. Then Kien cast in Big Tam's precious fishing net, and they waited. Loc leaned over the side of the boat to spot the darting fish below.

"There's one, Kien! There's another!" he shouted.

"You're going to fall in. Watch it!" Mai warned, but as she knew Loc was going to "fall in" a hundred times that day, she didn't much mind. They could all swim, and the day was warm. So what did it matter?

After a while, they pulled in a good netful of fish. Kien told Loc that he had helped a great deal and allowed the little boy to help lower the net a second time. Loc was in heaven, and Mai looked at Kien in surprise. Kien really could be, well, nice when he wanted to!

The second netful of fish was not as big as the first, but Kien didn't seem concerned.

"Let's take a rest, and we'll fish again later," he said. They lowered the sail and took turns swimming in the cool blue water. Before Kien jumped in, Mai saw him take something out of the pocket of his shorts. Sunlight glinted on the gold of Kien's precious wristwatch. Loc saw it too.

"What's that, Kien?" he shouted. "It's pretty."

"It's a gift," Kien said briefly, and Mai saw a

shadow cross the boy's eyes. Without saying another word, Kien shoved the watch out of sight.

Mai wanted to ask him more about the watch, but decided not to. Kien obviously didn't want to talk about it, and it was so easy to do nothing but swim and play in the water.

Later they climbed back into the boat and ate the good food Hong had packed for them—rice and salt fish, mangosteens and slices of papaya, finished off with small sweet cakes. They all ate so much that after the meal they lay down in the boat, Kien in the stern and Mai and Loc in the bow, and told stories as the boat rocked gently under them. Kien was telling an old folktale about a woman who turned into a mosquito, when Mai's eyes began to close. She tried to open them, but could not. The waves were so gentle and the sound of Kien's voice was drifting away. Drifting . . . drifting . . .

"Mai!"

Someone was shaking her. She came awake with a start and sat up in the boat. Where was the sun? And it was chilly! "What happened? Is it nighttime?" she cried.

"It's going to storm!" Kien was saying. He had started to shake Loc awake. "We've got to get the boat back to shore. We're drifting toward the sea!"

As Kien spoke, a wind seemed to come out of nowhere, pushing against the *Sea Breeze*. Kien hoisted the sail and the wind snatched at it so that it flapped and belled out. The *Sea Breeze* gave a sudden, sickening lurch.

"We've got to get back to shore," Kien cried. Where *was* the shore? Mai squinted into a suddenly all-gray world. The sky was gray, and the water, and the gray shoreline seemed very far away.

"Big Tam told me it might storm. I fell asleep and the boat drifted . . ." Kien began to sail toward the shoreline, tacking into the wind.

Loc, who was wide-awake, now, cried, "What'll happen to us when the storm catches us?"

A gust of wind answered him, causing the boat to heel to one side. Mai screamed. As if that were some sort of signal, the skies opened up and rain came sluicing down. With the rain came forks of lightning and more savage gusts of wind.

"Big Tam's nets!" Mai shrieked, as the precious net and all the day's catch of fish slid out of the boat and into the dark water.

"Have to . . . lessen the sail . . . or we're . . . done for!" Kien shouted over the roar of the rain and wind and thunder. "Help me, Mai!"

Battling gusts that threatened to overturn the boat, Mai followed Kien's orders.

"Are we going to drown?" Loc wanted to know.

"No, we won't . . ." But as Kien spoke, lightning sizzled out of the heavens. "That was close," Kien muttered.

Mai could see nothing but rain and grayness. Kien strained into this grayness as he battled the wind to reach shore. After a while, the wind changed.

"All right . . . this is good. It's taking us toward land!" Kien shouted as the *Sea Breeze* picked up speed.

Suddenly, Mai saw land coming—quickly. "We'll be wrecked against the shore!" she screamed.

"No, we won't." Kien swung the *Sea Breeze* out of the way of a jagged rock. Loc began to cry.

"I don't like the storm! I'm scared! I want to go home!" he wailed.

Mai knew just how he felt. But Kien was saying, confidently, "Don't worry, little brother. I've been in worse places. Look! Here we go!"

There was a sudden jar as the keel of the boat grated against something. Mai gasped. There was another jolt. Kien jumped out of the boat, standing shoulder-deep in water.

"Grab one of the oars. Row!" he shouted to Mai.

Mai began to row as Kien pushed the *Sea Breeze.* Another jolt, and then a long, grating sound that told her the *Sea Breeze* was grounded on sand. They were safe!

Mai's knees wobbled as she got out of the boat, pulling Loc with her. The three of them beached the *Sea Breeze.* "Where are we?" Mai screamed, over the storm.

"I can't tell. We're not near your village, anyway!" Kien yelled back. "Come on, help me push the old boat higher. If the storm pushes it back into the lagoon, Big Tam will tear off my ears!" Kien shook his head miserably. "It's my fault we lost his net. I fell asleep . . ."

"We all did," Mai consoled him. Kien shook his head unhappily.

"Big Tam trusted me to take care of you and the boat," he said.

They waited out the storm. It wasn't a long wait, for the storm died away almost as quickly as it had come. As soon as the skies cleared, Mai looked around her and was relieved to see some familiar landmarks.

"I know where we are," she told Kien. "Remember, Loc? Grandfather brought us out here last year. Let's look around. There should be a trail nearby that will lead us back to the Village."

It was not exactly a trail, but a series of marked

trees they could follow. Loc was exhausted, so Kien carried him piggyback, and he and Mai began to trudge through the thick forest. Watching carefully for the marked trees, they picked their way through a dense growth of bamboo, banana trees, and tangled lianas, the woody vines that always try to climb toward the sun.

"Your grandfather told me that there were trails through the forest," Kien sighed, as Mai deftly guided them through the trees and vines. "I wish I had paid more attention."

By the time the forest began to look familiar to Kien, Loc was fast asleep on Kien's back. They didn't talk much, for Mai was tired and Kien was busy trying to think of an excuse to give Big Tam.

"We're nearly at the vegetable patch," Kien finally said. "And there's the path farther on. Look . . . someone's come out to meet us. Probably Big Tam, ready to pull my ears off!"

"It's not Big Tam. I don't know who those people are," Mai said.

"Nor I . . ." Kien's voice changed. "Mai! Get back! Quick!"

His words woke Loc, who said sleepily, "What's going on? What's the matter, Kien?"

"We have to run back into the forest and hide! We have to get away before they see us."

But as Mai and Loc stared at Kien, two men and a women came into full view. Mai saw that they were strangers, and that they were smiling.

"Welcome back to the Village," the woman called. "We have been waiting for you!"

5

Mai and Kien stood still, waiting for the three strangers. One of the men was tall and thin, the other very plump. The woman was small and ordinary and wore gold-rimmed glasses, which kept slipping to the edge of her nose. When she smiled, her teeth showed —very white and sharp.

"Why, here you are," the woman said. "We have been worrying about you. You must be the three children who set sail in the boat this morning. We feared for you, in this storm."

Kien said, "The boat was wrecked. We managed to swim to shore." Mai looked at Kien, surprised at the lie. Who are these people? Mai wondered. Why is Kien afraid of them, and why would he lie about the *Sea Breeze*?

"We must get back to the Village," the woman was saying. "I am Guyen Thi Lam. This is Dao, and this is Hoa. We have been sent by the New Government of Vietnam to help your village. We are the first of many who will come to give you assistance."

She nodded to the two men, who walked around Mai and Kien so that they were in back. Sandwiched

"We have been sent by the New Government of Vietnam to help your village"

between the two men and Guyen Thi Lam, Kien and Mai began to walk past the vegetable patch and onto the path. Guyen Thi Lam turned around to smile at them, and Mai did not like the smile. The woman's teeth appeared sharp, like a shark's.

They were walking into the Village. Mai became uneasy. Something was wrong. The villagers were grouped in front of Grandfather's house, talking among themselves. Mai could see Hong, and Tam, who was hopping about on one foot and waving his crutch. There was Duc, too. But where was Grandfather?

"Where is the old man?" Kien asked the question for her.

Guyen Thi Lam turned her head to scowl at Kien. There was a hard look in Kien's eyes. "You mean Van

Chi?" she asked sharply. "He is in his house. He is a difficult man."

Mai opened her mouth to ask a question, then saw that Grandfather was coming out of his house. She began to run past Guyen Thi Lam, shouting "Grandfather!" He saw her, too, began to run toward her, then stopped.

"Mai . . ." he said, and the look in his eyes made Mai even more uneasy. He didn't look happy to see her.

She grabbed both his hands and held them tightly. "Grandfather, aren't you happy we're back?" He said nothing. "We went through a bad storm. Kien saved us."

"You are all right?" Grandfather asked, but slowly, his voice sounding strange and far away. He turned to Kien, who had come up with Loc on his back. "Is Loc all right?"

Kien nodded. Now Hong came rushing over, throwing her arms around Mai and scolding her as she hugged her.

"Mai, I am so glad to see you, foolish child, you've worried us to death! Heaven, you are soaking, and you too, Kien!" Loc, waking up and seeing all the people around him, blinked bewilderedly, and Hong added, "We were afraid you had drowned! It's Tam's fault for letting you go out on that boat. I told him and told him . . ."

"The boat has been wrecked," Guyen Thi Lam interrupted. Instantly, there was a silence. "It's a pity, because our Government could have had use for it."

Grandfather totally ignored Guyen Thi Lam. "Kien, the boat was wrecked?"

Kien nodded. "On the rocks, coming in." Why was he lying? Mai wondered. "I'm sorry, Tam."

Tam said nothing, and neither did Duc. Nothing, when they should have been very angry, or at least full of questions.

Mai whispered, "Grandfather, what's wrong? What's happening?"

Instead of answering her, the old man said, "Hong, could you please give Mai and Loc dry clothes?"

Instantly, Guyen Thi Lam said, "Our country has no masters and no servants. Hong, stay where you are."

Hong snapped back her wide shoulders and looked more like her old self. "Servant, you say? I'll have you know I'm no servant to this family!" she snapped. "I have been looking after these motherless ones for many years! Don't tell me the New Government disapproves of mothers!" She put one arm around Mai and another around Loc, and began to lead them toward Grandfather's house. "Tam, get Kien some dry clothes!" she shouted over her shoulder.

As if Hong's words had released them, the villagers began to talk loudly and started drifting toward their own homes. Tam put an arm around Kien's shoulders, and the two went inside Tam's house. Grandfather stayed where he was and began to talk to Guyen Thi Lam and the men.

"Hong . . . who *are* they?" Loc asked.

Hong said nothing. Once inside the house she suddenly burst into tears. "Hong, what is it?" Mai cried.

"They have found us!" Hong moaned. "All these years . . . and now they will spoil everything! You'll see!"

"Spoil what?" Loc asked, bewildered, but Mai thought of the woman's sharp white teeth and shivered. "Are they really from the . . . the New Government, Hong?" she asked.

Hong began to hand them dry clothes as she explained. "The war has ended. Vietnam is united under a new government. This new government is sending people like Guyen Thi Lam to all the villages. They teach people like us about the new government and its new laws." Her voice was shaking. "They have power, Mai. Guyen Thi Lam could tax us heavily. Or . . . or punish us if we don't agree with the Government's new laws."

"Punish us?" Mai whispered. "Oh, Hong, is Grandfather in some kind of trouble? Guyen Thi Lam said . . ." Her words trailed away as Hong met her eyes. Hong's eyes were very worried. Mai put her hands over her mouth and stared at Hong with wide, scared eyes.

"Let's run away," Loc urged.

"How? Where?" Hong shook her head. "There's no place to run to. *They* are everywhere, now!"

Just then Guyen Thi Lam poked her face through the half-open doorway. "Aren't you finished yet?" she demanded. "We are waiting. I have called a meeting of all the villagers."

Hong didn't answer her, but Mai nodded quickly, afraid to anger this woman. Taking Loc's hand, she hurried outside the house. The villagers were all there, standing or squatting in a semicircle around Guyen Thi Lam and the two men. The fat one, Dao, was saying, "The first thing we all have to realize is that we are friends." He smiled. "We are all going to work together for the good of our country."

Mai looked around for her grandfather and saw him standing in back of the villagers. Not far from him stood Big Tam. Mai did not see Kien at all.

"I'll take over, Dao," Guyen Thi Lam said, and the

fat man moved over quickly. Guyen Thi Lam smiled her shark's smile and said, "As Dao said, we are here as your friends. We'll tell you what our Government will do for you, and we'll also ask you to help the Government."

"Here it comes," Hong grunted.

"We've been told by your headman,"—the woman nodded toward Grandfather—"that this is a small and poor fishing and farming village. From what we've seen in other parts of the country, yours is a fortunate village. You have a buffalo, and you have fish from the lagoon, and vegetables from your field. You have a clever carpenter. War never touched you, so you've been living in peace all this time. Now it's time you helped the country. We're going to ask you to give a portion of your wealth to the New Government."

"How much is a portion?" Grandfather's voice was harsh, and Mai was scared for him, noting how angry Guyen Thi Lam looked.

"A portion is 50 percent. We want 50 percent of what you grow, what you fish, and of what your carpenter makes from wood."

"Fifty percent! That's half . . . half . . ." The sighing whisper rose among the villagers, and Duc bounced up to shout, "That's not possible!"

"Why is it impossible?" the thin man, Hoa, asked.

"Because . . . Do we look like such rich people? We just barely raise enough vegetables to eat! And with the *Sea Breeze* gone, how are we going to fish?" Duc spluttered.

"You built the first boat. You'll build another," Guyen Thi Lam snapped. "Now be quiet and listen!" Behind the squatting people, Big Tam made a loud, rude noise.

Mai could see veins throbbing in Guyen Thi Lam's neck. The woman was furious. She looked first at Grandfather, then at the villagers, and back to Grandfather again.

"Van Chi," she said, "you are a teacher as well as the headman here. I hold you responsible for the actions of these people."

"We have done nothing to be ashamed of," Grandfather spoke up. His voice was quieter now, but his face was hard and set.

"Is that so? We will see. You have taught the children of this village—and the adults too, I hear—wrong things for years. Because of you, they have the wrong attitude toward our new government." She turned to the villagers, sweeping them with hard eyes behind those gold-rimmed glasses. "That's all, for now. It is almost time for you to eat. After the meal, we will meet again, and I will speak to you all further."

Muttering and whispering, the group broke up. Tam turned to Grandfather, but the old man shook his head, as if he did not want to talk to anyone, and moved slowly down the path toward the forest.

"You! Van Chi!" fat Dao shouted rudely. "Don't get any ideas about running away, now!" The old man did not even turn around.

Now Mai saw Kien, sitting in the doorway of Tam's house. He was looking at her in a strange, thoughtful way, and she wondered if he would come over and speak with her. She wanted to ask Kien questions, since he had seemed to recognize and fear these strange and horrible people. But before Mai could call Kien over or go to him, she saw Guyen Thi Lam and Hoa, the thin man, walking toward her and Loc.

"This is your grandfather's house, is it not, little

ones?" Guyen Thi Lam said, smiling her white smile.

Loc nodded. "What do you want?" he asked. But the two strangers just pushed past Loc and Mai and went into the house. Mai, with Loc at her heels, hurried after them.

"What do you want in our house?" she cried.

"We feel that your grandfather is one of those who is against our New Government," Guyen Thi Lam said shortly.

"Grandfather never . . ." Loc began, but Mai hushed him.

"Loc," she hissed, "go get Grandfather. Go get him quickly!" Loc looked at his sister, then at Guyen Thi Lam, and ran.

The two strangers began to poke around the house. The thin man dumped Grandfather's black medicine bag upside down on the floor, scattering medicines and bandages every which way. Guyen Thi Lam seized the books.

"Nobody is allowed to touch my grandfather's books!" Mai cried in horror.

"I can see why!" The woman held up a fat book. "Do you know what this book is about? It is about people and countries who have been the enemies of our country!" She smiled at the thin man. "We've got him, Hoa!"

"Let him talk his way out of this," the thin man agreed.

Just then, Loc came racing into the house, followed by Hong. "Mai, Grandfather won't come, but Hong . . ." Loc stopped, and stared at the mess in the house.

Hong shrilled, "By what right do you do this, you? You say you're Government representatives! Well, I want no part of a government that acts like this . . ."

"Be silent!" Guyen Thi Lam thundered. She pointed a finger at Hong. "Your teacher and headman is a traitor! If you don't want to be treated like a traitor too, get out, and take those two brats with you!"

Hong turned bright red, then went ghost-pale. She took Loc's and Mai's hands, and backed out of the house.

"But, Hong!" Mai protested. Hong told her to hush.

"Don't say a word to anger that evil woman!" she whispered.

Now Guyen Thi Lam, Dao, and Hoa were grouped together, holding the book they had taken from the house. Mai looked toward where Grandfather stood. He was watching the three Government representatives, and his face was so angry and unhappy that Mai wanted to run to him. Hong held her back.

"Thay Van Chi!" Guyen Thi Lam said suddenly. "Do you admit you have been reading this book?" She held it up for everyone to see.

The old man sighed deeply. "It is my book," he said.

"You have taught these simple, good people from books such as these?"

"Yes, but . . ."

"He admits it!" Guyen Thi Lam shouted. "Villagers, your teacher admits his guilt! He admits to teaching you lies and wickedness!"

"I admit nothing of the sort. I taught the people to love our country." Grandfather's shoulders straightened. "It is you who lie . . ." He would have gone on except that, suddenly, a new voice spoke up, Kien's voice.

"But you did teach us bad things! You did!"

Mai gasped. Why was Kien saying this? Loc gabbled, "Mai, what's Kien saying? What's he saying about Grandfather?"

Guyen Thi Lam was almost purring. "Are you sure, boy?" she asked. Kien nodded. "There's your proof!" she said, in a satisfied voice.

"Liar! When it was Thay Van Chi who took you in!" Big Tam thundered.

"Be quiet!" Hoa shouted, and Kien said, "Don't pay any attention to them. The old man makes them afraid to say anything against him. They all think he has great powers, like a witch!"

How could anyone believe such lies! Yet Guyen Thi Lam, Hoa, and Dao were nodding their heads.

"Poor boy, you must have been badly treated by this evil old man," Guyen Thi Lam purred.

"Oh, yes, kind aunt, I was an outsider when I came here," Kien whined. "I had to go along with what everyone said, or they would beat me!"

"You are wise. And the Government won't forget you."

Mai waited for Heaven to open up and a thunderbolt to strike this liar, this evil and wicked liar, dead! But Kien went on smoothly, "I am an orphan. I have been hurt by the war. These people took advantage of me."

"Evil boy!" Duc shouted and jumped toward Kien. Hoa stopped him and gave him such a shove that Duc went head over heels in the dust. Hoa kicked Duc as he lay on the ground and would have kicked him again and again had not the woman said, "Enough! You heard what the boy said. It's not the fault of these simple villagers. The old man is to blame, and we're going to punish him." She turned to Grandfather.

"When we leave the Village, the day after tomorrow, you will come with us. We will reeducate you." A low wail began from the Village, silenced as the woman glared around her. "Who will go with him?"

No one spoke.

"Bring out the old man's books!" Guyen Thi Lam commanded.

Dao went into the house and brought out the books. He dumped them onto the ground. Then Hoa brought out a small flat can and squirted liquid all over the books.

"No!" Grandfather cried out. He ran to the pile of books and began, with trembling hands, to pick them up.

"Get away, old man!" Dao, smiling, pushed him aside. Thay Van Chi fell, picked himself up, and tried to get at the books again. This time, Dao hit him across the face, knocking him out of the way.

"Heaven sees what you do!" Mai screamed. She ran to Grandfather and put her arms around him as he lay dazed in the dust.

Guyen Thi Lam paid no attention to all this. She was striking a match, which she flung onto the pile of books. Flames leaped up and the books began to burn. Grandfather moaned aloud and Mai could not bear it. She covered her face with her hands, and then ran like a mad thing toward her house. The last thing she saw before she flung herself through the doorway was Kien, leaning forward to poke the books so that they would burn faster.

6

Guyen Thi Lam wanted the old man to make a public confession.

She and Dao came to their house after the book burning, and put it to him. "If you tell the Village that you have been wrong all these years, that you were wrong to oppose us as you have been doing ever since we came, we will not take you with us when we go," she said.

Mai held her breath. A part of her wanted to shout, "Don't admit anything!" But the sensible part of her knew that if only Grandfather would tell these horrible people what they wanted to hear, they would let him alone.

All Grandfather's anger seemed to have burned away with his books. "I can't lie to you," he said heavily. "I was never an enemy of the people." He touched his bruised face where Dao had struck him. "I never taught anything but the truth," Thay Van Chi added.

"You left the city to come here to this tiny village and poison simple people's minds," Dao said menacingly. "I will hit you again, if you continue to lie! You are an old man. You mightn't even survive the long miles we have to travel, or the resettlement camp in one of our new economic zones!"

Grandfather said, "You may beat me, but I cannot tell you lies. I left the city because first my son was killed in the war, and then my daughter-in-law died, bearing this one"—he touched Loc's head lovingly. "When I knew that the war was closing in on us, we left the city. We walked for weeks . . . months. Many times we were lost in the forest." He looked at Mai with a ghost of a smile. "Mai was a little girl then, but she was so brave . . ."

"We aren't interested in her bravery," Dao snarled.

"We might have wandered forever, lost in the forest, had the brothers Tam and Duc not found us. They took us back to their Village—a very small, remote Village. The people were kind to us, and Tam's wife, Hong, was like a mother to my grandchildren. I knew at once that I wanted to bring up Mai and Loc in this quiet, simple place where war had never come to hurt the people."

His voice was now a whisper, and there was so much pain in his words that Mai felt her heart break. She rested her cheek against her grandfather's thin old shoulder as he continued, "These were happy years, but I knew that someday they would end. People like you would come, bringing the senselessness of the world back to us."

"So you feel we don't have any sense!" Guyen Thi Lam got to her feet grimly. "You'll see how much sense you're going to get in the resettlement camp. You will stay here, guarded by one of us, till it is time for us to leave. No one will be allowed to visit you except to bring you your meals."

"We are all so sorry, Thay Van Chi. Why are they so cruel to you?"

The house became a prison. Though Mai and Loc could come and go as they wished, they refused to leave their grandfather. The old man seemed hardly aware of them. He sat in the house, staring at the blank spot on the floor where his books had been. He did not speak very much, and he didn't eat, even though the villagers smuggled in cakes and fruit for him. One woman even sent a handful of sweets in a brightly colored little bag. Hong brought it to him that night, weeping as she did so.

"We are all so sorry, Thay Van Chi. Why are they so cruel to you?" she whispered. "You are such a good man." She brushed aside her tears to add, angrily, "It's the fault of that boy, Kien. No, he's not a boy but a devil. I hope he will suffer for this!"

"Thoi dii . . . that's enough," the old man warned. "Don't ever wish evil against another, even to such a one as Kien."

Mai hated Kien even more than she hated Guyen Thi Lam and Dao and Hoa. She hated him because she had begun to believe that Kien wasn't such a bad person. The next morning, when she heard Kien speaking to Guyen Thi Lam in a sickly-sweet voice, she wanted to throw up. Kien was the only one in the Village allowed to go where he wanted and do what he wanted. The other villagers had to go about their everyday tasks, carefully supervised by Guyen Thi Lam and Hoa. Dao remained to guard the old man.

That afternoon, there was another meeting of the villagers. Guyen Thi Lam had the old man brought before all the villagers and made him kneel down in the dust.

"We have decided that 50 percent of what you grow and catch from the sea is enough for the Government," she told the people. "Tomorrow, Dao and I will leave this village, taking the Old One with us." A groan rose up from the villagers, and Guyen Thi Lam added sharply, "Hoa will stay with you to make sure you do as we instruct you. In a little while, many more Government representatives will come to this village. We will help you become a thriving, industrious village for the good of our country!"

Mai had thought and thought about Grandfather leaving the Village, and she could not bear the idea. It was as if a huge hand were grasping her by the neck, choking her. When Guyen Thi Lam had finished her talk, Mai went to the women and, pressing her hands tight together, bowed deeply.

"Please, kind aunt," she said in a very humble

voice, "a favor! Let me go with you when you take Grandfather away. He is so old and needs someone to take care of him."

"Who will take care of your brother?" Guyen Thi Lam asked, and Mai's heart leaped. Maybe she would be allowed to go with Grandfather! But then the woman went on, "The traitor Van Chi is getting what he deserves. Our Government doesn't punish children. No, you may not come with us."

Mai crept away. She felt so sick and sad she wanted to die. She could not bear to return to the house, even though she wanted to be with Grandfather. When at last she returned, the house was dark and Grandfather was finishing his packing. A small bundle consisting of a blanket, some medicines, and gifts of food given to him by the villagers stood by the door. On top of the bundle lay the little bright bag of sweets Thay Van Chi had been given the day before.

"I want you and Loc to have these," the old man told Mai in a perfectly normal voice. "I don't have very much to give you, Mai."

"Oh, Grandfather . . ." Mai wanted to cry, but it seemed as if the tears were all frozen inside her. "What will you do? When will they let you come back to us?"

Loc began to snuffle. "I will go and get Big Tam and Duc and all the men. We'll throw these bad people out of the Village!" he cried.

"No. If you do this, others like Guyen Thi Lam will come and all of you will suffer. It is better if they blame me alone." Suddenly, the old man knelt down between Mai and Loc and put his arms around them. "Loc, Tam and Duc came to see me a while ago while Dao was not looking. They wanted to do just as you said, but I wouldn't permit it. Instead, I asked them to take care of you, my grandchildren. Loc, don't cry. You will grow into a great fisherman like Big Tam! And, Mai—"

"Can I come in?"

Mai whipped around, saw Kien standing in the doorway. She couldn't speak as he came in swiftly, shutting the door behind him. "I don't have much time," Kien said.

"G-get out of here!" Mai stammered. She was so furious and so shocked she could hardly speak.

"Haven't you done enough?" Grandfather's voice was cold and hard. "Have they sent you to spy on me and my grandchildren?"

"Spy on you? Oh, I see." Kien grinned at them in his old, impudent way. "I did a good job of acting, I guess. Now we have to hurry. We don't have much time to get out of here. I bribed that fat Dao to leave me alone with you for half an hour . . . told him that I wanted to see you, even though Guyen Thi Lam had forbidden you to have visitors."

"But why . . ."

"You didn't think I really was on their side?" Kien went over to the bundle the old man had packed. "Good . . . bananas, cooked rice . . . even a container of water! We will need these, and that blanket. Come on, Mai, Loc . . . Uncle! We are going!"

Still, Mai could not move. She couldn't understand what was happening. "You helped them burn Grandfather's books!" she cried.

"Of course! They were going to condemn him as a traitor anyway, and it was my chance to make them believe I was their friend! How else could I help you escape?" He turned to the old teacher. "Don't you believe me?"

For the first time in two days, Thay Van Chi

smiled. "Yes . . . and I am glad. But we can't run away, Kien. They will catch us. No, I will go along with them in the morning."

"Uncle, you don't understand! Tomorrow, they will take you away. You won't survive their famous resettlement camp, I tell you! This is your only chance to get out of this place and be free."

"But they'll follow us and catch us."

"Not if we have a head start! You know the trails in the forest—they don't!" Kien said impatiently.

Mai began to plead, "Grandfather, listen to Kien! If those awful people take you away, I'm going to come to the resettlement camp with you!"

"Me too," Loc said.

The old man made up his mind. "Very well, we'll go," he said. "But where will we go?"

"There's a village east of here. If you can guide us there, Uncle, the people will hide us. They know me," Kien said.

The old man thought for a moment. "Very well. I know that Big Tam and Duc trade, sometimes, with a village to the east of us. I think I know how to get us there."

Kien picked up the bundle that lay by the door. "Don't make any noise and keep close to me," he ordered. "We'll soon be out of the Village and once we're in the forest, we'll be safe."

No one spoke as Kien opened the door and peered cautiously outside. The Village was silent and dark. Some distance away Mai could hear Guyen Thi Lam talking with Hoa. There was no sign of their guard, Dao.

"Come on!" Kien hissed, and they hurried down the path toward the forest. Mai couldn't help looking back at the Village. Good-by, she thought. Good-by, Duc, Big Tam, Hong. Dear, dear Hong, good-by . . .

"Be careful!" Grandfather was saying. "Now, I will lead. Follow me, all of you."

"We will follow you," Kien said. "Let's go now . . . quickly!"

Mai had never been in the forest at night. Long, long ago, when she and Grandfather and Hong had carried baby Loc away from the city, they had become lost. She remembered that dimly, but those faraway memories were nothing compared to how horrible the forest was now! Many times Mai nearly screamed as she tripped over sprawling roots that coiled like snakes. Once, a banana leaf brushed across her mouth like a cold, dead hand, and she did scream, startling birds that flew into the dark night, making some animal blunder away in the underbrush with a crashing sound. Another time, something slithered by her foot, and she stepped backward against Kien.

Grandfather said, "We have nothing to be afraid of from innocent animals."

But she was afraid, terrified by the sounds of the forest, the rustles of animals, the squeal of bats high overhead, the sharp clatter of palm leaves swinging in the night wind, and by the black darkness that was so thick she could not pierce it with her eyes no matter how she tried.

Loc didn't care for the forest either. "Can't we just go home?" he begged. "Can't we wait right here till those bad people go away and then go back to the Village?"

"Guyen Thi Lam said tonight that some 'representatives' would stay and live in the Village," Kien reminded him grimly. "Loc, we can't ever go home to the Village."

"Never?" Loc cried, and Grandfather said, "Not for a long time, anyway. Don't ask so many questions!"

In about an hour they had to stop. The old man was exhausted, and Loc, too, was tired. They found a clearing and spread the blanket, and on this small blanket all four huddled close together. Kien insisted that one of them should stay awake on watch while the others snatched a few moments' sleep. The old man said that he would take the first watch. Mai didn't believe she could ever go to sleep in such a place, but she was so tired her eyes closed at once. Before she fell asleep, she heard a murmuring sound in the distance and thought, The sea is nearby.

When she awoke, a grayish light was filtering through into the clearing. Beside her, Loc still slept, but the old man was awake and watchful.

"It's dawn," he told her. "We're safe."

"Kien?" she asked.

"He went to find water to fill our canteen. Are you hungry? Here is a banana."

Mai wasn't very hungry, but she took the banana. She had not taken more than a few bites when Kien came running back into the clearing.

"Wake Loc!" he panted. "We must get out of here!"

"What is it?" Mai cried, but the old man murmured, "They are after us!"

"Guyen Thi Lam and her people are beating the forest near us! There are many of them. I heard one of the men say that it was fortunate they arrived in our Village earlier than expected!"

Mai shook Loc awake as Kien repeated, "We must

get out of here before they come!"

"No, Kien," the old man said.

Kien was rolling up blanket, fruit, everything, into a bundle. "What are you talking about? Once we reach that friendly village . . ."

"Suppose *they* are in that village?" the old man asked quietly. "I feel it is useless, Kien."

"Why is it useless?" Kien cried angrily. "Don't talk like that! You act as if we should all give up and . . . and turn ourselves in to Guyen Thi Lam!"

"Not you . . . just me," the old man replied. "I will tell them that I forced you to come with me. I will take all the blame."

"Grandfather, no!" Mai cried, and Loc said, "What's going on? Why is everyone shouting?"

Mai saw her grandfather put his hand on Kien's shoulder. Kien looked as if he wanted to shrug off the hand as the old man spoke. "Kien, they will catch us. Perhaps they won't catch us today, or tomorrow, perhaps we will even escape them for a month. But then how will we live? Will we hide in the forest? The jungle? Will we go from village to village running away from them?" He shook his head. "We are going to find Guyen Thi Lam."

"You're insane!" Kien sputtered.

"No. I was selfish last night, when you came to the house. I wanted to believe we could be free. Kien, you once said I was living in a dreamworld. You are right. The country has changed, and there is no room in it for people like me."

"Then we will leave the country!" Mai cried.

"Leave . . ." Kien turned to look at her, and a strange light came into his eyes. "Yes," he said excitedly, "that *is* a way!"

"Now what are you talking about!" Thay Van Chi demanded.

Kien began to speak very quickly. "The *Sea Breeze* . . . don't you see it? We will leave on the *Sea Breeze*! If the country is too full of *them,* if they won't leave us alone, we will leave the country!"

"The *Sea Breeze* has been wrecked!" Grandfather protested.

"I lied! I didn't want *them* to get the *Sea Breeze*!" He began to walk about, so excited he could hardly talk. "Mai . . . Mai, you know the forest better than I. Are we anywhere near the place where the storm brought us? Are we anywhere near the place the *Sea Breeze* is beached?"

Mai forced herself to think calmly. "If we could find some marked trees, we would know," she said. "There were some that led back to the Village, remember? Those same marked trees will lead us to the *Sea Breeze,* if it is nearby!"

"Then all we have to do is find the trail, and then the boat, and we will leave the country!"

"I will not go!" the old man cried.

"Do you have a choice? Once they find us, that woman will not only punish you but Mai and Loc and . . . and me! I don't want to end up in some resettlement camp!" Kien began to run out of the clearing. "Mai, help me find the *Sea Breeze*!"

"The sea is close by," Mai murmured. "Let's look in that direction." She started to follow Kien, hesitated. "Grandfather?" she questioned.

The old man said sadly, "If it is true that you children will be punished, I have no choice. If we find the boat, we will try to reach Thailand. I can speak the language, and I have sailed the South China Sea and the

Thay Van Chi knelt down on the beach
and scooped some of the sand into the
little bright bag

Gulf of Siam. Perhaps, if Heaven is kind, we may reach Thailand safely . . ."

"Hooray!" Loc cried. "We're going to Thailand!"

It took them an hour to stumble upon the marked trees that led back to the shore where the boat was beached. During this hour they were terrified that Guyen Thi Lam and her friends might find them and drag them back to the Village. When they finally found the first marked tree, Kien let out a soft whoop of triumph and began running.

He reached the shore first and squatted by the boat, running his hands over its sides. "Good old boat, you waited for us!" he whispered. Suddenly he frowned. "Thay Van Chi, how can we sail to Thailand? We don't have any charts or compass!"

"There is a way to sail by using the stars and the sun to fix one's position. I know the winds and currents of the South China Sea, remember. But we have so little food—"

"There's no time to get more," Kien interrupted him. "Guyen Thi Lam may be right behind us."

The old man sighed. "I wish there was another way," he said.

"There isn't," Kien said, and Mai thought, This has to be a dream! I'm going to wake up back in the Village and Hong will scold me for oversleeping. At the thought of Hong, tears filled her eyes.

"We have food," Kien was saying, "and a little water. It will be enough."

"It will take us five days to reach Thailand. Four if we are very lucky," the old man began.

He was interrupted by a sudden rustle in the forest behind them. Far off, they could hear the sound of voices!

"They're coming!" Loc shouted, and Kien threw the bundle of food and water into the boat. As he did so, the small colorful bag of sweets rolled out of the bundle and fell on the ground. Thay Van Chi picked it up, and emptied the sweets into Mai's hand. Then he knelt down on the beach and scooped some of the sand into the little bright bag. He bent to kiss the ground.

"Hurry up!" Kien said, between his teeth. The rustling in the underbrush was coming closer. Now, they could hear the voices clearly.

The old man put the bag into his shirt, next to his skin. Then he looked at Mai and Loc, who were already sitting in the boat, and at Kien, who was waist-deep in water, waiting to give the boat a final push into the lagoon.

"We're ready?" he asked. Kien nodded. The old man waded out into the water and climbed into the boat. He set the sail, as Kien pushed the boat farther into the water, and clambered aboard himself.

"This is crazy," the old man said. "We are all insane."

"It's a crazy world," Kien said with some of his old impudence.

As the *Sea Breeze* drifted farther into the lagoon, Mai saw a group of people burst out onto the beach. There was Guyen Thi Lam, and Dao, and Hoa, and several others. Loc began to wave at them, mocking them.

"Good-by. I'm sorry you can't come with us!" Loc cried.

"Hush, Loc, please." Mai was terrified of Guyen Thi Lam, even at this distance.

The sails of the *Sea Breeze* filled with wind. Kien turned his face away from shore and began to sail the boat toward the China Sea.

"Good-by," Mai whispered, and as she did she saw Grandfather put his hand into his shirt to hold the little bright bag of sand.

VIETNAM

LAOS

THAILAND

CAMBODIA

HO CHI MINH
CITY

GULF OF SIAM

THE
VILLAGE

OUTCAST ISLAND

KUALA
LUMPUR

SINGAPORE

SOUTH CHINA
SEA

II
KIEN

The journey of the Sea Breeze

CAMELOT

7

Afterward, they would look back on that day and think, In the beginning it was almost an adventure.

They were grateful to be free of Guyen Thi Lam and her henchmen, who stood on the shore shaking their fists and shouting for them to come back. It was a beautiful day, warm but not too hot, with fair-weather clouds as a sign of a good sailing wind. Eagerly the *Sea Breeze* hurried to meet the China Sea.

"You will drown out there!" Guyen Thi Lam yelled after them. "You had better come back!"

"We'll have a better time out here than we would have in one of your camps, Auntie!" Kien shouted back. He was in fine spirits, and so was Loc, who made a rude noise and stuck out his tongue at Guyen Thi Lam.

"Grandfather, see how silly they look!" Loc shouted, but the old man sat in the stern of the boat without moving and just stared at the land. Tears filled his eyes—long, shining tears that slid down his cheeks. Mai, too, was near tears. She put an arm around the old man and knelt beside him in the boat. Seeing them, Loc looked uncertainly at Kien.

This won't do, Kien thought. If we all start bawling, we might end up by sailing back to Auntie Guyen Thi Lam!

"What kind of place is Thailand, Uncle?" he asked. "It must be a very fine place."

The old man said nothing for a moment and then nodded. "Yes, Kien. It is a fine place," he said. "I went there when I was a young man, and I remember how kind the people were." He tried to smile. "I saw elephants there, Loc, and there were bananas and coconuts and mangoes . . ."

"I am getting hungry," Loc said cheerily. "When will we get to Thailand, Grandfather?"

"You're always thinking about your stomach!" Mai's voice was sharp. Kien glanced at her, wondering if she was going to cry and sob. Mai hated leaving Vietnam nearly as much as her grandfather did. Well, you couldn't blame her. All she had known of Vietnam was the Village, that peaceful, silly little village.

Kien sighed. With him, things had been different. He had had no home, no family, and no one had cared much about him—certainly not the relatives who had left him in that orphanage!

Kien's nostrils flared at the remembered smells of hunger, too many unwashed babies, and crowded misery. The people who ran the orphanage had done their best, but there were so many orphans and so little with which to feed and clothe them. And then, Jim had come . . .

Kien automatically put his hand in his shorts pocket where he always kept Jim's gift, the watch. It wasn't there! Of course—he had given it to Dao! Kien suddenly asked himself why he had traded his precious watch for these three people in the boat. They meant nothing to him, and yet he gave up Jim's watch for them.

"Grandfather, is Thailand very far?" Loc was asking the old man.

"Quite far," the old man said sadly, and Kien was irritated.

"Look, Uncle," he snapped. "If you had bowed your head to Guyen Thi Lam and said what she wanted to hear, we wouldn't be out here in this old boat."

"Don't talk to Grandfather like that!" Mai flared. "It's not respectful."

"I suppose I have to be respectful to you, too?" Kien was suddenly sick of them all.

"Thoi dii . . . thoi dii . . . that's enough," Thay Van Chi told them both. "We are going to be on this boat for a while, and we must work together or drown together." He took Mai's hand. "You are angry at Kien because it hurt you to leave our country. Make peace with him."

Mai started to reply, then she sighed deeply. "You are right," she said. "I am sorry, Kien."

"Kien?" the old man now demanded, and Kien shrugged.

"I didn't start anything," he protested.

"Thoi dii!" This time, the old man's voice was sharp. "You have to act sensibly, too, Kien. This is no adventure but a deadly serious business. None of you have sailed on the open sea. I have. We can't quarrel between us. We must all work together and look after one another. We must be a family."

"Even Kien?" Loc asked.

"Kien also."

Kien smiled sourly to himself. Family, indeed, he thought. I suppose that means they've adopted me until we reach Thailand. After all, the old man needs me around to help sail the boat. How can he do it alone?

"So, now," the old man said, "we are going to have duties. Mai, you and Loc will take care of what supplies we have."

"We don't have many," Mai said. "Just the blanket, and the bananas and rice we brought with us from the Village."

"It will have to do till we reach Thailand." He dipped a finger into the sea and drew a map on the wooden side of the boat with his wet finger. "Here we are on the tip of Vietnam. Thailand is to the northwest of us. To get to Thailand we must sail through the Gulf of Siam."

"How will we find the way?" Mai asked in a troubled voice. "Do you know the way, Grandfather?"

"I have sailed these waters, Mai. I remember how to steer by the stars." He smiled at Kien. "Tonight I will show you how sailors can chart their course by using the stars and the North Star. During the day there is a way of using the sun to determine the position of our boat."

Mai looked satisfied, but Loc repeated the question he had asked earlier. "Grandfather, how far away is Thailand? How long will it be before we get there?"

"As I told you before in the forest, four, perhaps five days."

"And we aren't going to have anything to eat besides rice and bananas for five days?" Loc wanted to know.

"There's no way we can go back for supplies," Kien reminded him. "Look . . ."

Ahead was the spread of the South China Sea.

They all looked at the wide expanse of water. "It's so . . . big!" Loc whispered, and even Kien felt as if he

They all looked at the wide
expanse of water.
"It's so... big!"
Loc whispered

were shrinking, becoming as small as an ant in comparison to so much water. The China Sea looked calm enough, with the sun dancing over the water, but Mai shivered.

"Grandfather, suppose it storms?"

The old man did not answer. As the *Sea Breeze* slid out of the lagoon and into the sea, he fingered the small bright bag of sand.

They were lucky that first day. Good tail winds swept them along, and the sea remained calm and friendly, while the lagoon and the land mass of Vietnam dwindled into a shadow on the horizon. When the sun set that evening, it was so beautiful that Kien stopped steering the boat and even the old man stared. The sun seemed blood red, and the water and sky streamed with scarlet and gold. Later, the wind whipped up and the stars came.

The old man pointed out the North Star. "See? It

is constant, while the other stars swing around it. Sailors can use it as a base to steer by," he explained. "Loc, do you see the North Star?"

But Loc wasn't interested in steering by the stars. "Look how clear the stars are, Mai," he said. "Don't they look like the white butterflies we used to chase back at the Village? I remember Hong said—"

"I don't want to hear about the Village," Mai said in an odd little voice.

"Why? Grandfather, why doesn't Mai—"

"When we get to Thailand, we'll have a nice house, just as we did in the Village," Thay Van Chi said smoothly.

"In four days we'll have a nice house," Loc said. "And food," he added.

Kien's stomach growled. Loc wasn't the only one who was thinking of food. They had already eaten for the day—if you could call half a banana and a sip of water eating—but the old man had been strict about food. "Will you stop talking about food!" Kien snapped at Loc.

Again Thay Van Chi prevented a quarrel. "It's dark and you must all try to rest," he said. "I will watch and steer the boat while you sleep." He turned to Kien. "I will teach you how to steer by the stars, Kien, but for tonight, sleep, and relieve me in the morning."

They obeyed him without argument, Mai settling down with her head against the side of the boat. Loc snuggled down beside Mai. Kien made himself comfortable, propping his head on his arms so that he could lie down in the boat and look at the stars.

"Well," he murmured to himself, "we are on our

way to Thailand!" It was an exciting thought, a new adventure. I will always be free and looking for new adventures, Kien thought. How clever I was to find an old man who can steer a boat by the stars alone!

He wasn't really tired, but while he was thinking of his own cleverness and what a fine country Thailand was going to be, he fell asleep and dreamed of Jim.

He had not dreamed of Jim for months, even years. In the beginning, right after Jim left him that day back at the orphanage, promising someday to come and take him to America, Kien had dreamed of Jim every night, and cried himself to sleep again when he realized he had only been dreaming. Tonight, Jim looked exactly the way he had looked that day when Kien saw him for the first time.

"Hello, Kien boy!" the Dream Jim shouted. He was dressed in his Air Force uniform and was smiling widely. "You're looking good, son!"

"Have you come back for me, Jim?" Kien demanded. Then he shook his head. "No, I've given up waiting for you to come back for me, Jim."

The Dream Jim shook his head. "Don't give up on me, old buddy," he said. "I'll be back someday . . ."

"You're lying again!" Kien spoke up boldly. "Do you know how many weeks and months I waited for you? I sat by that squeaky old orphanage gate and waited each day. And every time that gate opened I'd run toward it, hoping it was you! But you lied, Jim. You were my friend and yet you lied to me. You never meant to come back for me. You never meant to take me to America."

The Dream Jim looked sad. "Kien, you're a survivor. You'll be all right. I'm sorry, Kien . . ."

Someone was shaking his shoulder, hard. "Kien,

I'm sorry," the old man's voice said in his ear, "but you'll have to wake up. I'm too tired to know what I'm doing. Besides, it's dawn."

Kien came awake, glad to be free of his dream. The sky was turning gray in the east.

"You sailed all night?" he asked the old man.

"Wake me if there's a change in either the wind or the weather," the old teacher said. He lay down in the bottom of the boat and fell asleep as Kien took the tiller, concentrating on the task of sailing. Jim, Kien thought bitterly, my friend Jim. He didn't want to remember how often he had cried himself to sleep, lonely for Jim. Even worse was the memory of how he had felt when he realized Jim would never come back. He had left the orphanage soon afterward, with petty cash stolen from the office till and food stuffed inside his shirt. He had lived by his wits ever since, and he had never had another friend.

Around dawn, Kien sensed a shift in the wind. It became stronger, and the air turned wet and heavy. He thought of awakening Thay Van Chi, then decided to let the old man sleep for a little while longer. He could handle things on his own, Kien thought.

About ten minutes later, heavy raindrops began to splash against the sails. At the same time, a gust of wind buffeted the *Sea Breeze,* spinning it around in a circle. "Thay Van Chi, wake up!" Kien called. "It's going to storm!"

They all woke up at that, Loc blinking as if he didn't know where he was. Mai said, "Storm? But we made it back to shore . . ." and Kien realized she was thinking of the storm they had sailed through a few days back.

But this was nothing like that other storm. Compared to a rainstorm in the open sea, a thunderstorm in the sheltered lagoon was like a fleabite compared to the bite of a cobra! As they stretched, another gust of wind smashed against the *Sea Breeze,* nearly capsizing it.

"Help me with the sail!" the old man shouted to Kien, as a third gust of wind spun them around again.

They battled with the sail, which flapped and tore out of their hands. They had not managed to haul it down when the rains came, smashing down on them as if they were insects to be crushed underfoot.

The boat crested a wave, pitched down into a valley between two swells. Mai screamed as the *Sea Breeze* heeled so close to the water that half of their food supply skidded across the deck and into the water. Mai nearly followed the food into the sea, but her grandfather grabbed her, pulling her back to safety.

"Hold on to the mast!" he shouted.

"I can't! I have to take care of the food!"

"The food doesn't matter. You'll be lost if you fall into that sea!" Kien looked at the furious water and grabbed hold of the mast with both hands. He made Loc do the same. There would be no way to rescue any of them from that mad water!

Pitching and lurching, up and down—there was no controlling the *Sea Breeze.* It was as if they were riding a horse gone mad. The boat would shoot almost vertically up a great swell, then ride down again into a valley between banks of water. Gusts of wind caught the *Sea Breeze,* turning it in a corkscrew motion, twisting and turning it yet again, until they were all sure that the boat would break up and fall apart.

Finally, the winds lessened and the rain eased. The storm had passed its peak. The boat still pitched and rolled, but the huge swells slowly calmed. Eventually

Kien seized the fish
and held it high
so that everyone could see

the sun came out, and they realized it was late morning. Now they could see what damage the storm had done.

"Almost half the food is gone!" Mai was in tears. "Most of the rice that is left has been soaked with seawater. I've managed to refill our water canteen with rainwater, so we have something to drink. But what shall we do for food?"

"Don't throw any of the spoiled food overboard," the old man advised. "I have an idea." He paused and added, "There's a much more serious problem than the loss of food. The storm has blown us off course, which means we've lost precious time."

"Even so, we're lucky," Kien said. "We could have gone down." He pointed into the dark water.

"Anyway, now we know that this old boat can survive a storm!" Loc pointed out happily. "And I know what your plan is too, Grandfather—we're going to catch fish and eat them. Isn't that right?"

Mai began to laugh. "I forgot all about the fish!"

"Don't ever let Big Tam hear you say so," Kien said. He was grinning, too. The sun shining down warmly on them made the storm seem farther away.

By afternoon, they had recovered most of their good spirits. The sails were not damaged, and a good wind blew from the east, taking them back on course. The old man found a fishhook stuck into the side of the boat, and making a string from woven strands of blanket, he produced an interesting-looking fishing line. The hook was baited with a kernel of spoiled rice, and they set out to do some serious fishing.

For a long while there were no nibbles, and though they took turns watching their precious line, there was no fish. Then, later that afternoon, Loc gave a yell.

"I caught one!" he shrieked. "Look, Grandfather

. . . Mai . . . Kien . . . I got one!"

A fat fish swung on Loc's line, wiggling and trying to get free! Kien seized the fish and held it high so that everyone could see. "Hooray for Loc, the wonderful fisherman!" he cried.

Loc was so proud he could hardly talk. "I'm so hungry I can eat the fish all by myself!" he cried. "I want it grilled."

Mai began to laugh. "Where are you going to grill it, silly? We don't have a fire in the boat!"

"You mean . . . you mean we have to eat the fish raw?" Loc squeaked. He grabbed the fish back from Kien. "Oh, no, you don't! You're not spoiling my fish!"

They were all laughing when the old man held up a hand.

"Listen!" he said in a hushed voice.

"What is it?" Mai cried, and her grandfather said, "I think I hear something!"

"Is it going to storm again?" Loc asked fearfully. *"Listen!"*

They held their breath. Now Kien could hear it, too. "It's a motor," he said, and the old man whispered excitedly, "A big ship is coming near us. If we can attract its attention, it will take us to Thailand!"

Loc jumped up in the *Sea Breeze* and began to wave.

"Here we are, Mr. Ship!" he screamed. Suddenly Kien caught his arm.

"No ship has a motor that sounds like that!" he cried. "It's a motorboat. I know!" Quickly he grabbed Loc and dumped him down into the bottom of the boat. "Quiet! Quiet for your life!" he hissed. "Those are pirates out there!"

8

"Pirates?" Thay Van Chi repeated, puzzled. "What could pirates possibly want with us? We have nothing."

"These pirates have no pity on anyone!" Kien was so scared he began to stammer. "I heard about them b-before I came to your village! They sail up and down the China Sea and attack all sh-ships and boats that pass!"

Now everyone could hear the sound of the motor. A dark speck had appeared in the east, and was growing steadily larger. "But if it is a boat, we should ask for help . . ." the old man said somewhat uncertainly. "Surely we can't survive another storm!"

"Don't you understand? Pirates help only themselves! Please, *please,* Thay Van Chi! I've heard horrible things about pirates . . ."

Kien's using her grandfather's full title impressed Mai. She said, "Supposing these are pirates. What shall we do?"

"Get down the sail! Hope they won't see us!" Kien started to pull down the sail, and after a moment Mai helped him. Loc boasted, "If there are pirates out there, they'll be sorry they ever saw us!"

"They don't have any pity on children either," Kien snapped. "I heard of one family . . . the pirates cut off a little girl's ears because her parents didn't have money."

Loc put his hands up to his ears in alarm. He looked at his grandfather, who said, "All right. Get down into the bottom of the boat and stay still. It's almost dusk. They won't see us."

But it wasn't that dark, Kien thought, as the *Sea Breeze* floated along under bare masts. The sound of the motor was very loud now, and the motorboat had come into clear view. Mai pushed Loc firmly down to the bottom of the boat.

"Let go, Mai!" Loc protested. "I want to see the pirates!"

"Just keep your heads down!" Kien begged. He had been in some tight corners before, but up till now there had always been some escape. In an ocean, there was no place you could run to. Kien prayed that the pirates would pass them by.

The motor was roaring as if it were no more than a few yards away. Don't let them see us, Kien thought desperately. He felt Mai's small hand give his a squeeze, and when he looked at her, he saw that she was smiling a little. Mai was trying to reassure him! But then, Mai hadn't heard some of the stories he had heard about the awful pirates.

A breeze rose and swept across the water, carrying rough voices. There was laughter, and then somebody began to sing. The roar of the motorboat was so loud it seemed to fill the world. Go *on,* Kien urged. Pass us by. GO!

Was it his imagination, or was the sound of the

motor moving away just the slightest bit? Kien peered cautiously over the side of the boat. He immediately pushed his head down, flat, on the bottom of the *Sea Breeze*. The pirates were right there! Not two hundred yards separated them from the *Sea Breeze*. How could they miss seeing the refugees? And when they did ... Kien shuddered. He had seen that one of the pirates cradled a wicked-looking machine gun.

But they were going. Merciful Heaven, they were going away, leaving a foaming wake behind them. A snatch of song drifted across to them, and that was all.

"Are they gone?" Mai whispered.

Kien couldn't say a word, but the old man replied,

Kien had seen that one of the pirates cradled a wicked-looking machine gun

"Yes, they have gone." He looked very pale. "You were right about their being pirates, Kien. I understood their talk. They were Thai pirates and they had just robbed a pleasure boat. I am glad you warned us in time."

"Won't they come back?" Mai asked, looking scared, but Kien had recovered himself enough to tell her that the *Sea Breeze* wasn't going to stay around to find out. The sail was hoisted quickly, and soon they were running before a good wind.

"Now, if it doesn't storm tonight, we will be all right," Kien said, looking anxiously at the sky. The sun had set and the world around them was turning dark. A pale moon had climbed into the sky.

"It won't storm again, will it?" Loc asked. "I don't like storms, Grandfather. Tell it not to storm!"

"Do you think Heaven will listen to me?" The old man smiled. "Perhaps I should go up to Heaven and demand fair weather, like the toad. Do you remember the story?"

They all remembered the story, but Thay Van Chi told it again, anyway. He explained how the ugly toad had led a group of animals up to Heaven to ask for rain during a drought.

"Grandfather, if the King of Heaven would do that for a toad, I'm sure he'd listen to you," Loc said thoughtfully. "It's worth a try, anyway!"

They laughed and felt better, and then Kien suggested that they divide Loc's fish. He felt hungry now that the pirates had gone.

The fish was about the nastiest thing Mai and Loc had ever eaten. Mai gagged over the fishy, raw thing, and Loc refused to touch his. The old man managed to swallow his share, however, and so did Kien. Thay Van Chi knew that they needed nourishment to live, and

Kien had eaten worse things.

"Don't throw anything overboard," the old man warned, as Loc was about to toss his uneaten portion of fish over the side of the boat. "We don't want to attract sharks. Besides, we can use the fish for bait."

Kien hadn't thought of sharks. He looked at the wide-open sea and suddenly felt a chill of fear. For the first time since leaving Vietnam he felt depressed. Pirates, raw fish, and now sharks too. I hope we get to Thailand soon, he thought.

He looked into the distance and saw that the horizon was smudged over by a line of dirty-looking clouds. Thay Van Chi, too, was watching the sky.

"That doesn't look good," he murmured. "It's going to storm again."

They fell silent, waiting. In a little while a cool wind began to blow across the water. The moon disappeared completely, and the world seemed inky black.

"It's starting to rain," Mai groaned.

"Let's hope that's all it does tonight!" Kien muttered.

The rainstorm that followed did not pack the violent gusts of wind that had frightened them so much the night before. There was no lightning. Sodden, sullen rain fell, and kept on falling through the long night and into the gray dawn. The old man steered through the darkness, even though there were no stars to steer by. "I am going by instinct," he told Kien. "I pray I am right."

Kien hoped so, too. Though no one had been able to sleep in the rain, they had caught catnaps, huddled in the bow of the boat. Toward morning, Kien heard the old man coughing. Everything in the boat was soaked. Rainwater had collected at the bottom of the boat, and washed against their legs. Everything was a sodden, chilly mess! Kien told Mai and Loc to start bailing.

Things went from bad to worse. Dawn was rainy, and there was mist so thick that they could not see ahead of them. Kien had no idea where they were going. Perhaps they were headed straight for a boatful of pirates! Perhaps they were near land and would crash against rocks! Kien felt tense and irritable, like everyone else on the *Sea Breeze*.

The day continued cool and dreary. Mai and Kien argued, and the old man snapped at them both. Loc whined. Evening came, and then night, still drizzly and cheerless. Had the moon and stars left the sky forever? Kien wondered. In pitch-darkness and grim silence, they nibbled a portion of the remaining rice, and half a banana each.

"There isn't much left," Mai sighed.

Kien glared at her through the wet dark. Did she have to remind them all how bad the situation was?

"I'm hungry," Loc grumbled. "I hate cold rice!" Kien wanted to tell Loc to shut up or starve.

How could anyone sleep? But they did doze off from time to time. In between times the old man coughed. He coughed so hard that Kien insisted on taking the tiller that night so Thay Van Chi could rest. The old man hesitated, then sighed.

"I suppose it can't do any harm," he said, and Kien realized with a sinking heart that they had been lost all along, that even the old man had no idea where they were.

"How long will the rain last?" Kien murmured to himself. "Has a hole opened up in Heaven?" As he sailed the boat, he seemed to be drifting into a dreamworld. He felt as if he had always been sailing in this miserable, wet boat. He tried to remember a time when he was warm and had a full stomach and dry feet, but he could not even remember such a time. He was so tired and so cold, and his empty stomach rumbled and growled and ached. After a long while he leaned his hands on his soaking arms and closed his eyes . . .

When he awoke, Mai was beside him. She had pushed him aside from the tiller and was steering. "You were tired, so I thought I'd do this for a while," she said.

He was ashamed of falling asleep, and he was wet and cold. "You don't know what you're doing!" he snapped at her.

"I know as much as you do right now," she replied at once. He had to admit that was true. She added, "Grandfather is finally asleep but he keeps coughing. And Loc is asleep. You should rest too."

"I'll be all right now," he said.

Mai handed over the tiller to him, and she added, "We're all going to be all right. We'll be in Thailand soon."

Kien wanted to say, If we're not hopelessly lost, but he didn't. Mai suddenly pointed.

"Look!" she cried. In the eastern sky glimmered a small but perfect star. "The rain has ended," Mai said joyfully. "Now we'll know where we are!"

Next morning, the welcome sun returned to beat down on them, bringing warmth and drying the sodden boat. The crew of the *Sea Breeze* lifted their faces to the sun, grateful for its warmth, until the old man insisted that they wrap cloths around their heads to avoid sunstroke.

"Drown one day, bake the next," Kien joked. The water seemed to pick up the sun's glare and reflect it at them, so that the heat, at noon, was almost unbearable.

They couldn't even go swimming, because sharks might be nearby. As the old man had warned Loc, these were shark waters. Although they had sighted no sharks, they had to be careful. Fortunately, yesterday's rain had left them plenty of drinking water, and thirsty from the heat, they drank a great deal. The old man, whose cough had worsened with the day, drank the most water.

Mai kept looking at her grandfather in a worried way. When Thay Van Chi refused to eat his portion of their last few bananas, she became even more concerned.

"Thailand isn't far off, Grandfather," she coaxed. "You must keep up your strength till we get there." But the old man would not eat anything, and when Kien brushed by him accidentally, he realized that the old man was burning with fever.

"You're sick," Kien said to the old man, who merely shrugged.

"It is nothing."

Later, however, Kien saw that the old man was taking something from his small store of medicines. It didn't help, and his cough became even worse.

The weather took a turn for the worse, too. Around sunset the sky clouded again and the worst storm of their three days at sea buffeted them. It began with a pelting rain that brought a vicious wind, and thunder and lightning that terrified them even more than the wind. Under bare masts, the *Sea Breeze* bobbed like a cork, up and down, up and down, while the crew sat petrified with fear. Though it lasted for only a few hours, the storm carried away all but two bananas and the canteen of water. They were almost without food.

And Thailand was still far away!

Next day they fished again, grimly this time, realizing that their aching stomachs would not be filled unless they caught something. When they caught their first fish, the old man ordered them to cut it up and use it for bait. Soon three more fish were caught, and this time even Loc ate. He gagged and nearly threw up, but the raw fish went down. Then they fished some more.

For nearly two days they existed on fish and rainwater. During this time the sea remained relatively calm, and periodic rains kept them supplied with drinking water. On their fifth day at sea, a huge white gull came to rest on their mast.

"That is a good sign," the old man murmured. "We will land in Thailand soon."

"When, Grandfather?" Loc wanted to know.

"One of these mornings you'll open your eyes and there the land will be, on the horizon," Kien said. He felt almost as cheerful as he had been when they first started out.

"Kien's right," the old teacher said. He reached out and gently touched Kien's cheek with his hot hand. So seldom had Kien ever been touched in this gentle way that he moved back, shocked. For some reason, he felt a strange uneasiness, even anger. I don't belong to you, Old Man! he wanted to shout. Just because I'm here with you and your grandchildren doesn't make me one of you!

Two days later, they sighted Thailand. The *Sea Breeze* by this time was limping along, nursing its wounds after the last squall that had battered it. The shoreline came upon them suddenly, a dark line on the horizon that at first looked like a shadow on the water. Then—there it was! Kien thought it was the most beautiful thing he had ever seen.

"Land!" he yelled, and Mai, seeing it, screamed too. "Oh, we are here! It's Thailand!"

Loc wanted to dive off the side of the boat and swim ashore, but his grandfather stopped him.

"The land is miles away, yet, and there are sharks in these waters!" he scolded. Then he began to cough and Mai begged him to sit down and rest.

"Let Kien do the sailing," she begged, but now that they were so close to land the old man would not let anyone else touch the tiller.

"Just think," Kien grinned. "We'll soon be on dry land. I can sleep in a bed that doesn't move!"

"And there'll be good food . . . rice and noodles and —and anything but fish!" Loc chimed in, licking his lips.

By now, they could make out a coast fringed with coconut trees. They could see houses beyond the trees.

"It doesn't seem as if we're coming to a great port," the old man said. "It seems like a very small town . . . perhaps even a village."

"Oh, look!" Mai cried. She pointed to a small motorboat that was making straight for them. "They've seen us! They've come to welcome us!"

Loc squinted. "There are one . . . two . . . three men aboard," he said. "Hello, Thais!" He began to wave wildly.

But none of the three men in the Thai motorboat waved back. They were all dressed in khaki uniforms and seemed to be officials of some kind. One of the men, a very fat man who wore a huge pair of sunglasses, now began to shout in Thai.

"What's he saying?" Mai asked. "Can you understand, Grandfather?"

The old man listened, and his face turned to a chalky gray.

"It is not possible!" he whispered. "They could not . . ."

"What is it?" Kien cried.

The three men in the Thai motorboat were now shouting together.

"Pai ban!" they were shouting. *"Pai . . . pai . . . pai!"*

"What does *pai ban* mean?" Loc wanted to know.

The old teacher looked from Mai to Kien, and then to Loc.

"They are telling us to go home," he said. "They want us to go away. They will not allow us to land in Thailand!"

9

Mai's eyes were very wide and scared.

"Grandfather, you couldn't have understood him!" she cried. "How can anyone send us away?"

Thay Van Chi's face was hard with anger and despair.

"There is no mistake. They don't want us to land," he said.

"But why?" Kien cried. "Why? What have we ever done to them? If they knew . . ."

"Pai ban, pai ban!" the fat man shouted, waving his hands. Kien felt like crying with rage. He wanted to jump into the water and swim out to the Thai boat. He wanted to hit the fat man.

"Please, Uncle," he pleaded with Thay Van Chi. "Tell them about us! Tell them about Guyen Thi Lam and . . . and the storm. Make them understand!"

The old man began to talk in rapid Thai, and the fat man, surprised to hear his own language, stopped shouting. Soon, however, he shook his head.

"Pai ban," he kept saying.

As the Thai motorboat drew alongside the *Sea Breeze,* one of the other Thais reached out and gave the

Sea Breeze a contemptuous push with his foot.

Mai began to cry. Loc, clutching his sister's hand, started to cry too. Kien glared at the Thai men as Thay Van Chi laid a hand on Loc's head and pointed back toward the sea. Kien noticed that the fat man looked a little uncomfortable.

"What did you say?" Kien breathed, and the old man replied, "I told him that if he sent us back out to sea, he would be murdering children. He is thinking about that now."

The fat Thai official had begun to perspire. He pulled a handkerchief out of his pocket and mopped his forehead. After a short discussion with the other two men in the motorboat, he said something in a surly voice.

"Ah," murmured the grandfather, pressing his hands together and raising them to his forehead in thanks.

"Is he going to let us land?" Mai asked breathlessly.

"Not yet. But he says we may follow him to shore. He will let us speak with the head of the village there. If the villagers will accept us, we may land."

"How could they not accept us?" Loc burst out. "They couldn't be that cruel!"

"It seems that many, many 'boat people'—that's the name they have for us—have left Vietnam and come to this part of Thailand in order to escape the New Government. The fat one is the chief policeman in these parts. He tells me that the community he lives in is poor. The people here are afraid that if more of us Vietnamese come to Thailand, there won't be enough food to go around."

"But we'd work!" Kien cried. "Tell them we'll

Kien had guided the boat to a wooden jetty

work very hard for you!"

"Perhaps we can convince the village chief of that," the old man said. "We must try to hope for the best."

He began to cough again, and Mai finally convinced him to leave off steering the *Sea Breeze* and try to rest. Kien took the tiller in silence. It was so different, he thought, from the landing they had planned and dreamed about. He glanced toward Thay Van Chi, who sat exhausted and unhappy, his head pillowed in his arms. This is a nightmare, he thought. I can't believe this is happening to us.

"Grandfather, look!" Loc cried. "Look, we're coming nearer to shore. There are coconuts in those palm trees . . . it looks just like home!"

"It isn't home, Loc," Kien told him. Maybe we have no home, he thought. We are boat people. He tried to push that thought away, but it clung to him, so he began to sing a song he had learned in the Village —a song about harvests and good rice, and buffalo, and home. After a while, Mai and Loc began to join in the song. And as they sang, they reached the shore.

By the time Kien had guided the boat to a wooden jetty in the Thai harbor, the men who had been in the motorboat were on shore and talking to a small crowd of people. The crew of the *Sea Breeze* looked over at these people, and one by one stopped singing. The Thais did not look friendly. Most of them were men, but two or three women stood near the jetty too. None of them smiled or made any welcoming gesture. The fat Thai policeman was talking to a man who stood a little apart from the rest of the people, an older man who was dressed in a white shirt and a checkered sarong.

"Is that the village head?" Kien asked the old man, who shook his head.

"I do not know," he said. "Whoever it is, he does not seem to want us, either."

As if in answer to the old man's words, the man in the checkered sarong now walked across the jetty and stared down at the crew of the *Sea Breeze*.

"Boat people," he said in heavily accented Vietnamese, "where do you come from? What do you want?"

"Bow! Salute him!" the old man hissed, and Kien, Mai, and Loc pressed their palms together, lifting their hands high over their heads as they bowed again and again.

"Honored sir," Thay Van Chi said, "we are a family. We have come from the southern tip of Vietnam, having lived in a village much like this one. We are poor people, trying to live a life of freedom. We felt that we could not live under the New Government in Vietnam." He paused. "Thailand means 'free land' in your speech, honored sir. We felt that here, in Thailand, we might be free."

The village head looked uneasy and shuffled his feet on the wooden jetty. Just then, a boy about Loc's age came running down the path to the jetty. He was eating what looked like a mango.

"Oh, mangoes!" Loc groaned. "Oh, I'm hungry!"

The village head pretended not to have heard Loc, but one of the women in the crowd seemed to understand what Loc meant. She was a tall, thin woman, and something about her face reminded Mai of Hong. Stepping forward, the tall, thin woman spoke to the policemen in a sharp voice.

The policemen shook their heads, and the fat official said something in an angry voice. The woman stepped backward into the crowd, but she kept her eyes on Loc.

"Grandfather," Loc said, his hands pressed over his empty stomach, "can't I swim to shore and get some mangoes? Please?"

Thay Van Chi turned back to the village head. "Sir, you see how things are with us. My grandchildren are so young. We have come so far! For a week, now, we have been at sea. Storms nearly wrecked our boat. We had only a little food, and we have eaten raw fish and had only rainwater to drink." The old man would have said more but he began to cough violently.

"You are sick!" The village head said in an accusing voice. "We don't want to catch any bad Vietnamese diseases."

"My grandchildren are not sick," the old man gasped. "Please, take them!" He shoved Loc and Mai and Kien forward. "They will work. They are good children. I am old and it doesn't matter about me."

The village head now turned to the people behind him. They looked uncertain, but soon some of them began to mutter and shake their heads. The thin woman put her hands on her hips and said something under her breath. Then she stepped back and began to walk away from the jetty.

"They will not let us stay," Kien groaned in despair. "They are going to send us away!"

The old man fell down on his knees and knocked his head against the bottom of the boat. Mai and Loc stared at their grandfather, and Kien felt sick watching the proud old man beg for their lives.

"I plead with you in the name of Heaven!" Thay Van Chi cried. "Do not send us back to the sea to die!"

"Grandfather . . ." Mai began uncertainly, but Kien grabbed her and Loc and fell on his knees, dragging them down with him.

"Do what he does!" he hissed. "It's our only chance!" In a beggar's whine he cried, "Honored sirs, honored sirs, be pitiful and don't send us out to die!"

The village head looked very uncomfortable indeed. He said, "It is a law we have made. At first, we took in every Vietnamese boat person who came this way. We let them sleep in our homes, and we gave them food before they went to a refugee camp. But so many came that we became poor because of the Vietnamese. Why should we go hungry to feed you?"

"We would work," the old man groaned, but the village head turned his back on them. "Surely your government cannot know you are sending us away?" the grandfather cried, in despair.

The village head snapped, "We are a small village. We make our own laws. Why don't you go to a big city like Bangkok? See if they'll let you land there! The people are rich there, and they may take you in." He was getting angry. "Why do you bother us? We didn't start your war. We don't have anything to do with your new government. We don't want any part of you!"

The old man remained kneeling at the bottom of

the boat, his head pressed on the damp boards.

"Go away before we push you back to the sea," the village head said. One of the men on the shore picked up a pebble and threw it at the boat. It hit the side, making a dull noise. Other men shook their fists at the *Sea Breeze,* and the fat policeman shouted, as before, *"Pai, pai . . . pai ban!"*

"At least, let us have food and water!" Kien begged.

"No, you must go now. We have no food to spare!" the village head cried. "If we let you come ashore, you'll run away and hide, and we will never find you. I know how tricky you boat people can be!"

"We aren't leaving till we get some water and food!" Kien said. An anger had begun inside him, and it was ballooning through him until he felt his heart would burst with rage.

The village head said something to the men on the shore. A few of them jumped into the water and began to wade, waist-deep, toward the *Sea Breeze.* Kien picked up an oar and waved it menacingly.

"Come closer and I'll hit you!" he shouted.

"I'll help you, Kien!" Loc grabbed an oar, too.

"No . . . no!" Thay Van Chi lifted his head from the bottom of the boat and tried to stop them. "They are many, we are few. There is no use . . ."

The villagers now were at the side of the boat. They began to push the *Sea Breeze* into the water.

"IUT!"

The command in Thai came so loudly that the villagers stopped pushing and Kien stopped in the act of bringing down his oar on the head of one of the villagers. They all looked up onto the jetty. The tall thin woman was standing there, accompanied by some other women. All of them were carrying things—a bunch of bananas, a handful of mangoes, a few coconuts. The tall woman was holding what seemed to be a whole roasted chicken.

Seeing the food, Loc dropped his oar and cried, "Oh, food! Food! Oh, food!"

"It can't be for us!" Mai whimpered. Seeing the food sent saliva into her mouth, and her empty stomach began to ache unbearably. The old man said nothing, but held out his hands in a pleading gesture.

The village head was shaking his head violently and arguing vehemently with the tall, thin woman. She ignored him, stepped out onto the jetty, and beckoned for the *Sea Breeze* to move closer to the shore. The men wading in the water looked at one another, shrugged, and stepped away as Kien and Mai rowed closer to the jetty. The tall, thin woman handed down the food.

Loc was the first one to get food. He grabbed a mango, seized it in both hands, twisted it and pulled it apart. Then he sat down to slurp the fruit joyously in blissful silence. Mai tore the chicken apart, handing a drumstick to her grandfather and the breast and a wing to Loc. Kien took the other drumstick. Then, Mai, too, began to eat.

"Aah . . . *dii mak, dii mak,*" the thin woman murmured, and Mai looked up to see tears in the woman's eyes. She wished she knew how to say thank you in Thai, but the woman understood, for she nodded and turned away.

Now other women were handing down tin cans full of a brownish liquid.

"Tea for your cough," Kien said to the old man, who sipped at the liquid.

For a while they ate in silence. It had been so long

since they had eaten anything but raw fish that they even forgot their main problem. But they were reminded of it when the village head interrupted their eating.

"Now, you go!" he snapped.

Mai was shocked. Somehow, after seeing the tears in that thin woman's eyes, she had thought . . . She turned quickly to her grandfather, who said, "Is there nothing we can do or say to change your minds?"

"We have given you food we need ourselves," the village head replied sullenly. "Take it and go."

Mai looked desperately at the thin woman who was standing near the jetty. On an impulse, Mai fell on her knees and grabbed Loc's hand.

"Take my brother! Take Loc!" she cried to the thin woman. Sadly, the thin woman turned away. Now Mai knew that they had lost.

Kien had taken an oar in his hand and was beginning to row. His eyes smarted with angry tears, but he was not going to cry before that village head or that fat Thai policeman! The group on the jetty watched as the *Sea Breeze* headed again for the open sea.

"Those bad people!" Loc cried. He turned to his grandfather. "You said it would be all right after we reached Thailand. You said so, Grandfather! But the Thais are bad people!"

"They are not bad," the old man said sadly. "They are just afraid. They are afraid that our coming will hurt them somehow."

No one said anything for a long time. At last Mai lifted her chin resolutely.

"Where to now, Grandfather?" she asked.

Kien looked at her with surprise and respect. Mai had spunk, he thought.

The group on the jetty watched as the Sea Breeze headed again for the open sea

The old man did not reply for a long moment. Then he sighed.

"Where?" he asked. "I do not know. It is a miracle that our small boat survived the sea to reach Thailand. Where else could we go?"

"Try a new Thai port, maybe . . ." Kien suggested.

"No. They would only push us out to sea again," Mai said. Her chin went even higher. "You've sailed these waters, Grandfather! You know all about the countries around here. How about going on to Malaysia? Or Singapore?"

"Do you realize how many days we'd have to travel to reach any of these places?" Thay Van Chi asked. "We might be turned away again." He began to cough. "We should try . . . to return . . . to Vietnam . . ."

"No, Grandfather! We will find someplace. Heaven will take care of us," Mai cried. Help me, her eyes said to Kien, and Kien made himself smile.

"Sure, Uncle," he said with a touch of his old impudence. "I'll go anyplace but back to Auntie Guyen Thi Lam!"

Nobody laughed. Nobody said anything. Silently the four sat as the *Sea Breeze* slowly returned to the open sea.

10

It was as if they had always lived on the sea. Their feet had been chilled forever by the cold water that washed into the boat. Their faces, shoulders, and arms had always been scorched by the sun—the sun that also cracked their lips and made drinking painful.

They had always been hungry, it seemed. The food given to them by the Thai women lasted six long days. They ate the chicken first, because it would spoil, and then the mangoes, one by one. The green bananas had turned brown before they were devoured, but soon they, too, were gone.

They kept the coconuts for last, sharing first the milk of a coconut, and then the sweet white meat. Nibbling at the fruit bit by bit, they made each coconut feed all four of them for a day. It would have been easier if they could have caught some fish, but the fish were wary of the hook they let down into the sea and none were caught. By the time they were down to their last coconut, all of them had lost a great deal of weight, and the old man was very sick.

Thay Van Chi tried to hide this from the others. He made a joke of his cough, saying that it was his old lungs' way of reacting to clean sea air. But Kien and Mai could see how the fever burned in him, so that his eyes were almost glazed with it.

On the sixth day after leaving Thailand, Kien heard the old man whisper, *"Toi chong mat . . .* I am dizzy."

Kien's heart squeezed with fear. The fever was getting worse, and there was no medicine, no food, and no port in sight. Supposing the old man died . . .

Kien quickly tried to push the thought away, but it kept coming back. Suppose the old man died? He was the only one who knew these waters, and it was he who was piloting the *Sea Breeze* toward Malaysia. He had all the maps locked inside that wise old brain . . . the brain that was burning with fever!

What happens, Kien asked himself, when the Old One can't think straight anymore?

He looked over to where Mai was trying to coax the last bit of coconut into the old man. "Please, Grandfather, you need to eat," Mai was saying.

"I'm not hungry." The old man shook his head stubbornly.

"But you have to eat!" Mai was near tears.

"You eat it, Mai. You need it more than I do. Why, you're skin and bones."

This was true, Kien thought. Well, all of them were like that now. Mai's cheekbones stuck out like ridges under her skin, and the hand that held the piece of coconut trembled from weakness. Looking at the food, Kien couldn't keep his empty and aching stomach from growling loudly.

"Give it to Loc," the old man said. "Or Kien."

Kien shook his head, but Loc started to put out his hand eagerly. After a moment, however, he drew it

It was as if they had always lived on the sea

back. "No, Grandfather," he said with a great effort, "you haven't eaten your share. I have."

"And I never liked coconuts." Kien forced himself to joke. "You eat, Uncle. Anyway, we need to have you strong and healthy. How could we reach Malaysia without you?"

The old man seemed to realize that Kien spoke sense. He took the piece of coconut and began to chew the white meat. After a while he began to cough again, and when he spat over the side of the boat, Kien was sure he saw blood. If Thay Van Chi's sickness had reached the lungs, it was really bad. Now Kien was very frightened.

To make things worse, it stormed that day. It had rained off and on since they had left the Thai village, and they were grateful for the rainwater, which they could drink. But this was a storm like nothing they had yet experienced. It began as a darkness gathering swiftly on the horizon and then spreading across the sky. Although it was only just after sunset, the world seemed completely wrapped in darkness. The wind began, and the *Sea Breeze* commenced to lurch and pitch.

"This one will be bad," Thay Van Chi warned. "We had better lower the sail immediately."

"Will it be as bad as that first storm?" Mai worried, but her grandfather didn't say anything. "Worse?" Mai faltered.

"Let's hope not." The old man was making an effort to help Kien and Mai with the sail. "We have gone through a great deal, my grandchildren. Heaven will help us through this storm."

No one said anything. They waited for the storm, listening to the fierce sound of the wind blowing across the sea. Soon the black and sullen sea was heaving, and it began to rain. Tons of water, suddenly released, came foaming down on them. Wind shrieked across the bare mast, making the boat heel first to one side and then to the other, turning and twisting it without mercy. The force of the wind was so tremendous that Kien, clinging to the mast, was nearly torn loose and thrown into the sea.

Thay Van Chi leaned close to Kien and bawled something in his ear. Kien couldn't hear. The old man shouted, "Tie Loc and Mai and yourself to the mast! Use the rope from the sail!"

Kien knew that if they were blown overboard, they would drown. There was no way they could hope for rescue. But to get the rope from the sail he needed to let go of the mast himself. Kien was afraid to let go. Suppose, he thought, I am blown into the sea?

"It's all right . . . it's all right . . ." the old man shouted. "I'll hold on to you. I won't let you go!"

The old man wrapped one arm around the mast and hooked his free hand into Kien's shorts. Kien looked at the frail old arm and thought, If he coughs and weakens, he might let me go. But at the same moment a wicked wind rocked the boat, and Loc was torn loose from the mast. Mai screamed, but her voice was carried away by the wind. Kien, without thinking, let go of the mast to catch Loc and haul him away from the heaving water. Only when Loc was safe did he realize that the old man's grasp on him was sure and strong.

"The rope!" Thay Van Chi shouted over the storm, and Kien began to tug the rope free from the sail. "Don't lose the sail!" the old man ordered, so Kien ended up by wrapping the sail around the mast first. Then he began to tie Mai, Loc, and himself to the mast.

"Tie Grandfather too!" Mai screamed, but the rope was too short. Kien had an idea.

"Hold hands . . . all of us hold hands!" he bellowed, as the wind snarled and shrieked around them. He grabbed Loc's hand with his right hand and the old man's with his left. Mai held Loc's free hand and her grandfather's. Then Mai began to scream.

"Look!" she wailed. "Look . . ."

The *Sea Breeze* was poised at the top of a monstrous swell that was as high as a mountain. Down below was a valley of water. As they slid down into that valley, Kien closed his eyes. He popped them open a second later and screamed, too, as he saw black, hungry, foamy water waiting for him an inch away. It rushed into the boat with such force that they could not breathe.

We're drowning . . . we're going, Kien thought, and then the boat shot up another swell. Up, down, up . . . there seemed to be more water inside the *Sea Breeze* now than outside! Down, up, down . . .

"We're going to die . . . We're going to die!" Mai began to scream. Loc was howling, but his open mouth made no sound above the roar of the rain and the wind and the sea. "We're all going to die!" Mai shrieked.

Over the noise, Kien heard a new and strange sound. The old man was leaning next to him and he was speaking. No, he was singing! Kien stared at the old man, thinking he had gone crazy, that the storm had driven him insane. But the gentle old eyes were clear, and it seemed to Kien that Thay Van Chi was smiling.

Kien could hardly hear the words of the old man's song, but he soon recognized snatches of the melody. It was the Vietnamese song that they had all sung six days ago when they sailed into the Thai port. The half-recognized melody made Kien's eyes sting with tears as he remembered good rice, and laughter, and forests, and everything else he had taken for granted. He began to sing too.

Now Mai stopped screaming to listen. And she, too, began to sing. Loc, exhausted and limp against the mast, grew quiet as the others sang the familiar words. Some of the horrible fear lessened. It was as if Thay Van Chi was saying, The storm will soon be over, and the good things we've had before are waiting for us.

Their voices never rose above the storm, but they could hear each other sometimes, and it made them feel better. They clung to each other's hands and sang and sang. After a while even Loc began to sing.

It was dawn before the storm finally subsided. It had stormed for hours. Long ago they had stopped singing and now they slumped, exhausted, against the mast. They hardly knew the storm was over as they half rested, half dozed. The *Sea Breeze* sloshed with water taken on during the storm, and the hair that fell across Mai's face, hiding it as she slept, was wet too. Neither she nor anyone else saw something huge and dark pass them in the dawn light.

Aboard the tanker *Casa Verde*, Ramirez was just coming off duty. It had been a bad night and he was tired. He was also very hungry, though just a few hours before, his stomach had been lurched around by the stormy sea.

Now that sea seemed so calm. Looking around at the water, Ramirez suddenly stopped, stared.

"Eh, Felipe!" he shouted to another crewman who

Neither Mai nor anyone else saw something huge and dark pass them in the dawn light

had come off duty with him.

"Now what's wrong?" the other man asked anxiously.

"Do you see what I see? To starboard . . . over there!" Ramirez pointed, and his friend frowned into the gray dawn.

"I see a boat with people," Ramirez said.

"Um," Felipe nodded. "Vietnamese boat people, I'd say. No one else would be crazy enough to be out in the middle of the ocean in a little fishing boat. I'm surprised the storm last night didn't finish them off."

"I'd better get the skipper," Ramirez said, but as he was hurrying off the deck the other man stopped him.

"Don't do that, Ramirez. You know the skipper didn't get much sleep last night. He wouldn't want you waking him on account of some boat people."

"But we can't just leave them out there," Ramirez said, shocked.

"Who asked them to leave Vietnam in their miserable little boats?" Felipe retorted. "Listen, you know what the policy of our company is. We take no boat people aboard. It prevents a lot of embarrassment and trouble. No country wants those refugees anyway, and we can't support them all, can we?"

Ramirez looked over his shoulder, for the dark shape of the fishing boat was now behind him. It bobbed up and down in a forlorn way. Ramirez cleared his throat. "We could let the skipper decide," he began uncertainly.

"*You* call him up here. I don't want *my* head chewed off! I'm going to get some hot coffee!"

Ramirez remembered how hungry he was. The thought of hot coffee made his mouth water. But before he followed Felipe down into the galley, he looked once more at the fishing boat, now far behind the *Casa Verde*.

It's not my fault they're out there, Ramirez said to himself. Shrugging, he went down to breakfast.

11

When they awoke, arms and legs stiff and sore from clinging to the mast all night, it was well into day.

The sun was blazing down on them and had already baked them dry. The sea had calmed, and gentle swells lifted the *Sea Breeze,* moving it back and forth. Kien came awake first, and then Mai. Loc snored loudly, but the old man leaned forward against the mast, his face hidden by his thin arms.

He was so still that Mai was afraid.

"Is he . . ." she began, and Kien reached over and shook Thay Van Chi, who muttered but did not awaken.

"He's all right," Kien said. He felt sick with relief. "We got through the storm all right!"

Will we get through another one? Mai wondered. "Kien, Grandfather's very sick!"

"I know that! What can I do?" Kien's voice was high with frustration. "What can any of us do? We have to get to Malaysia, that's all!"

"The storm must have blown us off course," Mai sighed.

Kien knew this more than anyone, but Mai's

words made him angry. "What good is it to talk to you? According to you, we should jump overboard and end it all . . ." He stopped, staring into the water. "Oh . . . no!"

"What now?" Mai demanded.

"Look!" Roughly, Kien grabbed Mai's arm and shook her. "Look!" he repeated.

Near them, floating lazily, were two dark triangles that rose above the water's surface.

"Sharks!" Mai screamed.

Her scream woke Loc.

"Sharks?" he asked confusedly. "Has Big Tam brought home a shark?"

The old man awoke, too. "Sharks?" he muttered dazedly. "Where are the sharks?"

Kien pointed out the triangular dorsal fins. "They know where to find their dinner," he said shortly.

"But how did they get here?" Mai pushed her clenched fist against her mouth and her eyes were enormous with fear.

"Who knows? They don't wait to be invited. These are shark waters and the sharks are the tigers," Kien replied.

Thay Van Chi started to speak but could not, for coughing. Finally he managed to gasp, "Don't bother them . . . and they won't bother us. Don't throw anything overboard . . . and *don't* fall into the water!"

"Will they eat me if I fall into the sea?" Loc demanded, with his eyes bigger even than Mai's.

"In two gulps! Mai, help me hoist the sail," Kien said. "Thay Van Chi, how far off course are we?"

By some miracle the old man knew. By calculating when the sun was at its highest point, he figured out their latitude and told Kien that he felt they were not too far off course. "In three days, if we're lucky, we should sight Malaysia," he said wearily.

Kien looked at the old man worriedly. Would he be able to hold out for another three days without food —three days during which there might be another storm? Would any of them be able to hold out? He glanced over his shoulder at the dorsal fins slowly circling the boat and shivered.

They dined later on rainwater collected from last night's storm. There was no food left, and when Loc tried to fish, there was no bait, and no fish. Perhaps the sharks had scared away the fish. Thay Van Chi sighed as Loc brought up his fishhook in despair.

They had been hungry before. Now they were starving. They filled their stomachs with water till they bloated, but this didn't help. Kien, who was a little stronger than the rest of them, felt bone-tired. It was an effort even to keep hold of the tiller. The old man slept all the time and so did Mai and Loc.

Once the old man awoke and said, "Perhaps we may somehow stray, by Heaven's mercy, into a shipping lane. That may well be our only hope."

"What is a shipping lane?" Kien asked, and Loc opened his eyes to look at his grandfather hopefully.

"A shipping lane is the path great ships from many countries travel as they sail across the ocean. Many ships use the same 'lane.' If one of those great ships saw us and rescued us, we would be saved . . ."

"Then let's pray for a big ship!" Loc murmured weakly. He staggered to his feet, placed the palms of his hands together and lifted them to his bowed forehead.

"Please, Heaven," he said earnestly, "send us a big ship."

The sound of Loc's voice awakened Mai. She said, "It's no use. No one will ever come."

There was a big lump in Kien's throat as Thay Van Chi whispered, "Don't talk like that, child. Come to me." Mai rested her face against her grandfather's chest and cried. Kien could see Mai's shoulders moving with weak sobs, and he wanted to cry too. Instead, he began to whistle the song they had sung during the storm. His whistle was weak, but in a little while Loc picked up the song, beginning to hum softly. Mai and the old man listened, and Mai stopped crying. She lay quietly, listening, with her arms around her grandfather's neck.

Look, Heaven, Kien thought in his heart, look how hard we are trying! Can't you help us . . . just a little?

It was hours before they heard the noise. At first no one paid much attention, for they were too tired to do much but doze. It was close to sunset, and the sky was just beginning to turn gold and scarlet. At first, Kien, who steered the boat, thought it was the sound of distant thunder that he heard. Then Loc gasped, "I think I hear something."

They were awake and listening instantly.

"I don't hear anything—" Mai began sadly.

"Shh!" Kien interrupted her urgently. "Yes! I hear it too! I hear it too!"

"A ship!" Loc screeched.

They all peered into the distance.

"Look!" Kien shouted. On the horizon was a dark speck. "Look!" he cried again.

Loc was beside himself. "A ship, a ship!" he cried. Weak as he was, he jumped up and down in the boat. "I knew Heaven would send us a ship! I knew it! Look, Grandfather, look Mai . . . a ship's coming to save us, just like Grandfather said!"

The dark speck was moving closer, growing larger. Loc waved wildly, and so did Kien and Mai.

"Here we are, Ship!" Mai screamed hysterically. "This way . . ."

"Get *down!*"

Kien was seized, hurled to the bottom of the boat. As he lay there too surprised to move, the old man pushed Mai and Loc down too.

"Pirates!" Thay Van Chi gasped. "Be quiet . . . for your lives!"

Pirates! Kien nearly stopped breathing. Of course! He should have known that no large ship would run so noisily. This had to be a pirate's motorboat.

"It's too small to be a cargo ship or a tanker!" The old man groaned. "Pray that they haven't seen or heard us!"

But they had been seen. The motorboat was headed straight for them! Kien pushed the tiller hard, trying to turn the *Sea Breeze* so as to outrun the motorboat. It was no use. Kien saw several men standing on the deck of the large motorboat, which now swooped around the *Sea Breeze,* causing the smaller boat to pitch and yaw. These men cradled machine guns in their arms, and several of them waved and shouted at the *Sea Breeze.*

"Boat people . . . Stop . . . We won't hurt you!" one of them shouted in bad Vietnamese.

Kien looked at the men and shuddered. All the pirates had cruel, greedy faces. He looked at Mai, who was sitting stone-still, too frightened to cry.

"Don't anger these men," Thay Van Chi said rapidly. "Be brave. We have nothing to steal. Maybe they will leave us alone . . ."

With pirates, Kien knew, there was no "maybe."

All of the pirates had cruel, greedy faces

Every horrible story he had heard about these evil men came back to him. One of the pirates, a small man with the most wicked-looking face Kien had ever seen, leaned over and grabbed the side of the *Sea Breeze*, bringing it close to the motorboat. Then he sprang aboard the *Sea Breeze*.

"Boat people, where you go?" he asked, smiling. The smile made him look even more evil.

"We are trying to reach Malaysia, honored sir," the old man said in a shaky voice. "We are very poor people. My grandchildren and I have nothing except the rags we wear . . ."

There was a shout of disappointment from the pirates. "Where is your food? Don't you have any clothing . . . blankets?" the evil-faced pirate demanded angrily.

"We have nothing. We lost everything in the storms . . ." Thay Van Chi began to cough. The evil-faced pirate began to shake the old man.

"You're lying! You've hidden things! I know you boat rats!" he shouted. "Give me what you have or I will kill you!"

"Let go of Grandfather!" Loc cried shrilly. He broke away from Mai and ran over to the pirate, pummeling him with his small fists.

There was a shout of laughter from the other pirates. "Hey, Boon, can't you handle the Vietnamese puppy?" one of them yelled. This made the evil-faced pirate angrier still.

Kien saw the rage in those wicked eyes and acted quickly.

"Honored sir," he babbled, "pay no attention to my bad-tempered little brother! He has had brain fever. He doesn't know what he's doing."

"Yes, please . . . He doesn't even know his own name!" Mai added swiftly. She fell on her knees. "Let us go," she pleaded. "We have nothing . . . nothing at all!"

With an angry cry, the wicked-looking pirate shoved Thay Van Chi away from him. The old man fell on his hands and knees and stayed there, too weak to move. Then the pirate lifted the machine gun he carried. There was a blast of sound, and Kien cried out, thinking he had been shot. But the evil-faced one had only fired at their sail, peppering it with bullets. Now he blasted away at the mast of the *Sea Breeze*. The mast snapped, falling into the sea.

"Shall we sink the boat, too?" the pirate shouted to his friends.

"Why? It's a waste of ammunition, Boon! Just throw their oars overboard. They won't last long anyway."

Kien could not believe what he was hearing. The pirates were going to let them go! He watched dazedly as the evil-faced one threw the *Sea Breeze*'s oars overboard. Then he turned to go. Kien almost said a prayer to Heaven. But suddenly, as swift as a cobra, the pirate spun around, grabbed Loc, and hopped back onto the motorboat!

"Mai!" Loc shouted. "Grandfather . . . help!"

Mai screamed, and the old man jumped to his feet. "Pirate dogs!" he cried. "Give us back the child! Give him back . . ."

The motorboat began to move away.

"Follow them!" Thay Van Chi shouted.

"How? They've snapped the mast and shot the sail to shreds and we have no oars!" Kien was almost sobbing. "Give Loc back, you . . ." He tried to think of a name bad enough, but could not. "Give the boy back!" he yelled.

The leering pirate grinned. "You want him back that much? Well . . . catch!"

Kien saw Loc's face—shocked, surprised, scared— a second before he was flung into the air. Loc shrieked once, then fell into the water with a loud splash some two hundred feet away from the *Sea Breeze*.

"Swim, Loc!" Mai screamed, and Kien thought, The sharks!

The old man was about to leap into the sea to get Loc, but Kien dived first. He did not even think as he moved, only saw Loc's small head surfacing, and the dorsal fins of their shark escorts moving toward Loc. Then Kien was knifing through the water, swimming desperately. He saw Mai standing in the *Sea Breeze,* her arms around her grandfather. He heard the pirates' mocking laughter as their motorboat sped away. He swam faster and faster still.

Now he had reached Loc. Loc was too dazed to swim, but he struggled as Kien tried to drag him to safety. "Quit that, you fool!" Kien gritted. He couldn't see the sharks anymore. The big tigers must be hunting under the water.

Hurry . . . hurry! Kien felt something sandpaper rough brush against his leg. He did not dare think of what might happen if the shark opened its great jaws and snapped at that leg. He swam, stroke by stroke. The great burst of strength that desperation had given him was gone. He was exhausted, his lungs burning. Again, the sandy thing bumped against his leg.

Now he was almost within reach of the *Sea Breeze.* The old man was half in and half out of the boat, reaching for them. Kien sobbed once with fear as he pushed himself to the very limit. He was almost there, almost . . .

And then the old man was pulling both Loc and Kien into the *Sea Breeze.* Kien hardly felt the bottom of the boat as he tumbled in and lay gasping for breath. He hardly realized he was still alive.

Nearby, he could hear Mai saying Loc's name, over and over and over. "Loc, oh, Loc . . ." Mai whispered.

"He's fine," the old man said.

"The pirates . . ." Kien couldn't talk much, and the

old man seemed to understand.

"They've gone, my child. Now you must rest. Breathe. Breathe deeply. Put your head down so, below your knees. Breathe. Breathe."

"That shark almost got us." Incredibly, Loc seemed almost boastful. "I felt him brush my leg! I hope that shark eats up those wicked pirates!"

Mai shivered. "Don't talk like that!" she said sharply.

They were very silent as the sun suddenly sank. Then Kien roused himself wearily. "Our mast is gone, and our sail . . ."

"I saved the sail," the old man said. "See? It is beside the boat. I need your help to pull it out of the water, for it is very heavy." He paused. "Also I have saved the oars. The waves pushed them toward the boat."

So now, Kien thought, we have to row our way to Malaysia!

Pulling the soaking sail out of the water took Kien's last remaining strength. As dark fell, he rested his face against his drawn-up knees and closed his eyes. He must have dozed, for when he awoke, it was inky dark, and Mai was sitting beside him.

"Grandfather and Loc are asleep," she said quietly. "You've been asleep yourself for a long time."

"No one's sailing?" Kien asked and then caught himself. How could you sail a boat without a mast? "We have to make repairs," he muttered. "But . . . how? Where?"

Mai didn't seem to hear his question. "You were so brave, jumping after Loc like that," she whispered. "I was a coward. I wanted to go after Loc, but I couldn't move . . ."

"I didn't know what I was doing," Kien said truthfully. "If I'd stopped to think about that shark, I would never have jumped in."

"But you saved Loc. There's no way I can thank you." Mai's voice drifted away, then came back. "Grandfather tried to see where we were by the stars —they were out a little while ago—but he isn't sure. He thinks we're still on course for Malaysia." She paused. "He's getting so weak, Kien, and those pirates upset him so. He needs help, and medicine. He needs a doctor."

Kien didn't answer. He felt frustrated and helpless, and he wanted to scream at Heaven, to curse it. Instead, he picked up one of the oars the old man had saved and dipped it into the sea. Mai did the same. Where are we rowing to? each could have asked, but neither one did. It was better to do something—anything—than to sit and wait to die.

Together, they rowed for a while. Kien tried not to think of anything, but his hunger-weakened brain filled with images: the shark, and Loc, and the old man's face bending over him, and the old man's voice calling him "my child." He thought of the way the old man had begged for his life back in Thailand. My life, Kien thought. No one has ever begged for me before.

Land, he thought desperately, within himself. I want land for this old man. Can't you hear me, Heaven? I, Kien, want land!

The night slipped by. Too weak to row for long, both Kien and Mai fell asleep at their oars. The old man slept, and Loc slept, too.

When dawn came, Mai was the first to open her eyes. She raised her head and looked around her blearily, first to the west and then to the east.

"Kien!" she gasped. "Kien, wake up!" When he did not move, she shook him violently. "Kien, tell me I'm not dreaming!"

Kien woke up, and he too stared.

Ahead of them, feathered with palm trees and looking better than their best hopes and prayers was—LAND!

12

They stared at the land, afraid that if they spoke or moved it would disappear. Mai whispered, "Is it real?"

"It's real," Kien replied in a shaky voice.

Mai began to clap her hands. "Loc! Grandfather!" she shouted. "Wake up! Wake up!"

Loc staggered to his feet, but the old man lay where he was, bent forward, his head propped up against his knees. Kien bent down quickly and took the frail wrist in his fingers. To his relief there was a faint pulse.

"He'll be all right, now," he said to the others. "We'll be able to get help for him."

Loc was staring and staring at the land as if he was afraid it would disappear. Then he whispered, "Maybe they won't let us land."

"They'll let us land!" Kien cried. He felt as if he could knock down anyone who stood in their path. "Let's hurry and get there!" he shouted to Mai and Loc. "Grab an oar!"

The dark landmass slowly became a fringe of green trees that stretched halfway across the horizon. There were rocks jutting out suddenly from the blue water that surrounded this land, so Kien sent Loc to kneel in the bow of the *Sea Breeze* and warn them of any rocks he might see under the water. Loc had sharp eyes and often he warned, "Be careful! There's a flat rock to the right." Or, "There's a nasty one near you, Mai, so take care!"

Through the noise of this splashing journey, the old man was very still. Kien did not tell Mai and Loc how worried he was. Once when he was traveling from village to village he had seen a very sick man slip into a deep sleep from which he never awakened. Supposing the old man . . .

No, Kien told himself. Heaven can't be so cruel! Not now, when we're so near land! He said aloud, "Where do you think we are, Mai?"

"Malaysia?" Mai wondered out loud. "Perhaps Grandfather was mistaken when he said we were off course. Could that storm have pushed us closer to Malaysia than we thought?"

Loc said he didn't care—land was land.

"Oh, Mai! I see coconuts on those trees!" he shouted. The thought of food was almost unbearable to Loc, and he licked his lips. "Hurry up, can't you? I want some coconuts!"

Now they were close enough to see the details of a long sandy shoreline edged with dark rocks and tall coconut trees. There was no sign of people.

"Good," Mai said grimly. "I don't want to see anybody, not until we land anyway! Once we're on shore, *nobody* is going to push us off!"

Kien laughed. "You tell them, little sister!" he teased.

In a short while, they heard the wonderful sound

"Oh, Mai! I see coconuts on those trees!"

of the *Sea Breeze* scraping on sand.

Land! Land! Their long voyage was over.

Kien jumped into the water, waist-deep, and started to push the boat ashore. Mai and Loc paddled furiously, helping him. Kien was almost delirious with the joy of having solid ground under his feet, and Mai, unable to wait to feel this too, jumped off the boat and helped Kien push. Gradually the good old boat was beached.

"It brought us all the way here!" Mai was almost sobbing in gratitude. "Oh, I wish Tam could know!"

Kien nodded silently. Then he shouted, "Loc! Loc, what are you up to?"

Loc streaked by them and tumbled onto the sand. Without a word he sprinted from the palm trees that were growing nearest the shoreline. Climbing like a monkey, he slithered up a palm tree and reached a coconut. He twisted it off, and heaved it straight at Kien.

"Stop that!" Kien howled. For answer, Loc threw another coconut. "Do you want me to come up there and make you stop?" Kien shouted.

"I'm just getting our dinner!" Loc called back. He was having the time of his life. Down came two more coconuts.

"Thoi dii... enough! Remember Grandfather!" Mai cried. Kien grabbed up one of the coconuts, and finding a sharp rock, began to hack off the hard outer covering that hid the sweet milk and white flesh. This wasn't easy. The coconut was green and tough. Once Kien had managed to gash out an opening, he handed the coconut to Mai, who hurriedly clambered back into the *Sea Breeze* and held it to the old man's lips.

Thay Van Chi was barely conscious, but he managed to sip some of the coconut milk. Meanwhile Kien had hacked open a second coconut, which he shared with Loc. When Mai had finished feeding her grandfather, Kien had a third one opened—for her. The three of them sat down on the sand and tore their coconuts to pieces, chewing greedily on the sweet inner flesh.

Loc wanted to eat more, but Kien wouldn't let him. "You don't want to get sick. We haven't eaten for too long!" he warned. Now that he had eaten, he felt strong enough to add, "Mai, help me get the old man off the boat and into the shade over there."

They half carried, half walked Thay Van Chi off the *Sea Breeze* and onto land. The old man revived enough to murmur "Where . . . where?"

"We found land, Grandfather!" Loc shouted. "We've reached Malaysia!"

The old man shook his head weakly. "Not . . . Malaysia . . . too far away . . ." Then he began to cough weakly.

They made him sip some more coconut milk and then laid him down under a shady palm tree. Kien told Mai he was going for help.

"I'm coming with you," Mai said quickly.

"But we can't leave your grandfather and the boat," Kien argued.

"Loc can stay here with them. It will be all right. No one will bother them," Mai told him. "Hurry, Kien. Grandfather needs help now!"

Kien looked around him. From where they stood he could see nothing but palm trees and more palm trees. It did not look as if anything or anyone harmful was about. But to leave Loc alone . . .

"I don't know," he muttered.

Mai shrugged impatiently and began to walk away toward the palm trees.

"I want to come too!" Loc cried.

Kien sighed. "I know you do. But someone has to stay with the old man and the boat! That's important!" He took the little boy by the shoulders and shook him gently. "You must stand guard and make sure no one harms your grandfather or the boat. Do you understand, Loc?"

Loc nodded, impressed by Kien's grave tone. "All right," he said. "If I see or hear anything, I'll yell. But you won't be too far away?" he asked anxiously.

"No, we won't go far."

We can't go too far, Kien thought, as he followed Mai. His legs felt weak and rubbery after so much time at sea and so little food. Mai walked slowly too, and Kien caught up with her before she disappeared among the coconut palms that fringed the shore. These trees did not grow close together, as did the trees in forests they knew back home. Instead, each seemed to be rooted in the sandy soil as if it had staked a claim to a certain spot of land. Kien began to mark the palm trees as they walked, using a sharp bit of stone. "Otherwise we'll get lost," he told Mai, who nodded.

"I wish there was some kind of path," she said. "Do you think anyone lives here?"

"Of course! They must!" But after they had walked for some time, Kien began to wonder. It was so quiet, and there seemed to be nothing about but sand and coconut trees. Once a great white sea gull scared them silly by flashing out of a nearby palm tree. That was all.

By the time they had walked for about half a mile, both Kien and Mai were exhausted.

"Let's rest a minute," Mai panted.

"We can't. We need to get help for the old man," Kien told her.

So they kept on walking. Slowly, and then still more slowly they moved through the palms. It was disheartening. There was nothing—nothing at all!

"Not even fresh water," Kien groaned.

But he was wrong. Just as he spoke, Mai pointed. "Look!" she cried.

A short distance away, there was a clearing. In the middle of the clearing, ringed by rocks, was a shallow pond. Mai and Kien moved closer, and Kien stuck a finger into the water, tasting it.

"It's fresh all right," Kien said. "It's probably rain-water that collected here."

"So we have fresh water, anyway," Mai sighed. She sank down near the pond and rested her head against one of the rocks that surrounded the water.

"Fresh water, and nothing else. I'm sick of sand and coconut palms!" Kien looked around him and shook his head. "What a little nothing of an island!" he burst out.

"Kien! Just last night you'd have given your right arm for land, any kind of land!" Mai said.

"You're right," Kien admitted. "But how are we going to get help for your grandfather? Nobody seems to live here." He stopped, as Mai's face paled. "What's the matter?" he demanded. "What's wrong?"

"Look!" Mai breathed. She pointed to something caught in the rocks by the pond.

"So what?" Kien demanded. "It's just a bit of cloth that . . ." He stopped, then, and slapped his knees hard. "Cloth! So there *are* people! We just have to find them, that's all!"

Just then, far off and faint, came a sound. Kien looked at Mai, and Mai at Kien.

"Was that Loc?" Mai breathed.

They held their breath, listening. In the extraordinary stillness of the place, they seemed to hear the noise again.

"Let's get back to Loc and your grandfather—fast!" Kien cried.

Following the trail Kien had marked, they hurriedly backtracked. Though they were worried and afraid that something had happened back on the beach where they had left Loc and the old man, they were so weak they had to stop and rest many times. During one of these rest stops Mai held up a hand.

"Listen! I *know* that's Loc!" she breathed.

Kien listened intently. Sure enough, he too could hear Loc calling—"Mai! Kien!"

Now they did not rest anymore. Pushing aside their weariness, they hurried along until they burst through the palm trees onto the beach. There they both stopped and stared, and Mai gasped.

Loc and the old man were not alone. A half dozen men were standing around the *Sea Breeze*. One of them, a tall man with a bit of rag tied around his bald head, was talking to Loc. It was this bald man who turned toward Kien and Mai as they stood staring.

"Welcome," he called. "Welcome to Outcast Island!"

"Who . . . ?" Mai stammered, but she could say nothing more. Loc hurried over to her.

"Oh, Mai! What do you think? These people are our friends. They are Vietnamese, like us! And there is a doctor who has been examining Grandfather. He's gone to get medicine so that Grandfather can get well."

Kien grabbed Loc by both shoulders.

"Slow down!" he ordered. "What's going on here? Who are these people?"

The tall bald man walked over toward Kien and Mai.

"My name is Bác Thong . . . Uncle Thong," he said. He had protruding teeth, and this, together with his unusually round eyes, gave him a comical appearance. "We are Vietnamese, as this little one says."

"Are we back in Vietnam?" Mai gasped.

"No, little sister, that's not where you are at all!

We are boat people, like you. But you were luckier than we. Our boat sank out there." Bác Thong jerked a thumb at the sea. "We struck a rock during a storm, and half of our people—all of our women, in fact—were drowned."

"That is why we have called this miserable strip of sand and palm trees 'Outcast Island,' " a big fellow behind Bác Thong said. He spat on the sand. "We have been here for months now, dreading the arrival of the monsoons. Spending monsoon season on this pile of rocks will be as bad as spending it out on the sea."

"Ahn always complains," Bác Thong said with a loud laugh. "Come, Ahn, you'd much rather be here than at the bottom of the sea, wouldn't you?" He paused as a little, important-looking man came hurrying through the palm trees. This newcomer carried a small black bag.

"There's our doctor!" Bác Thong shouted.

Mai heard the word "doctor" and forgot about everything else. She hurried after the little man, who squatted beside Thay Van Chi.

"Will he be all right?" she whispered.

The doctor said nothing. He examined the old man, pulling a stethoscope from the black bag.

"Don't worry," Bác Thong reassured Mai and the others. "Dr. Phan Tri is an excellent doctor. He was in charge of a hospital back in Vietnam before the Viet Cong overran our city. Luckily, we even saved some of Dr. Phan Tri's medicine when our boat was wrecked. That medicine is like gold here on Outcast Island, but we'll share it with you."

"That's not all we'll have to share," the big man, Ahn, muttered. "I suppose we'll have to feed these people? More fish to catch, that means!"

"We'll work—we'll all work," Kien put in swiftly, and Bác Thong glared at the big man.

"Ahn, keep quiet. Your tongue runs away with you," he snapped. "These are our guests! They've been through hard times. Where is your sense of decency?" He turned to Kien with an apologetic smile. "I'm sorry about Ahn. He tends to be bitter." He put an arm around Kien's shoulders and drew him aside. "The little one says that you sailed that boat all the way from the southern tip of Vietnam. He says that the Old One needed neither compass nor map—that he has all the maps in his head!"

"He is a wise old man," Kien said. He looked worriedly at Ahn, but the big man had turned away and was busy examining the *Sea Breeze.* "Bác Thong, I am sorry to . . . to make extra trouble for you."

"What trouble?" the bald man cried. "We are all from the same country, aren't we? We have to help each other."

"Yes, indeed," one of the men standing around the *Sea Breeze* now said. "What we have is yours."

They were all smiling at Kien, even Ahn. Kien felt humble and grateful. "I will work . . . We will do anything you ask," he mumbled.

"You are a fine boy!" Bác Thong rumbled. "Come, Dr. Phan Tri! What do you say about the old man? Is he going to live?"

The doctor, who had been pressing his ear against Thay Van Chi's thin chest, now straightened. "He has pneumonia, Bác Thong," he said gravely. "He is an old man and has been weakened by exposure and starvation."

"Can he be cured?" Bác Thong asked worriedly. He really cares, Kien thought, and Mai looked anxiously at the little doctor. "Can't you use your penicillin tablets?" Bác Thong went on.

"You know we don't have many penicillin tablets left, Bác Thong!" Dr. Phan Tri protested. "I really think we should keep those pills for us . . ."

"You do as I say!" Bác Thong ordered. "This old man must be cured! You give him penicillin!"

The little doctor nodded grudgingly, and dipped into his black bag, bringing out a small bottle. Inside the bottle was a handful of pills. "As you wish, Bác Thong," he grumbled.

Mai pressed her hands over her face, so grateful she could not speak. Kien, however, whispered, "Our thanks, Bác Thong, for this old man's life."

"We'll take him back to our camp," Bác Thong ordered. "A wise old man such as this, a man who can sail without a map or compass, must not be allowed to die!"

Mai asked, "Is the camp very far?"

"Not far at all. Come, you, Ahn, and you, Tich, and Tranh—help carry the old man," Bác Thong ordered. Three men immediately lifted Thay Van Chi, and with the doctor walking alongside, hurried between the palm trees. Mai followed, with Loc at her heels. Kien, however, hesitated.

"What's the matter?" Bác Thong demanded. "Aren't you coming?"

Kien felt foolish. "It's the boat," he said. "I . . . I don't like leaving the boat."

Bác Thong winked his large round eyes. "Ah, you are a boy after my own heart. I know how you feel, for when my boat was wrecked out there I was very unhappy too."

"You see," Kien tried to explain, "the Sea Breeze is

damaged. I—I feel strange about leaving her here, unattended."

Bác Thong dropped an arm around Kien's shoulders. "Don't you worry, lad. Nothing will happen to your boat. Tomorrow I will tell my people to help you mend the *Sea Breeze.*"

Kien was truly overwhelmed. For the first time in his life he didn't know what to say. Finally, he stammered, "You are too good to us, Bác Thong."

Bác Thong's prominent teeth glistened in his smile. "Why? Because I help you? To confess the truth, you really cannot stay here too long. Ahn was right when he said we'd need to catch more fish and work harder to support the four of you. So it is to our best interests that your grandfather get better, that you go back on board your mended boat and take to sea again. Do you see?"

Kien nodded. That certainly made sense, though he didn't look forward to putting out to sea again. As if reading Kien's thoughts, Bác Thong gave Kien a friendly shake.

"Meanwhile, you'll rest, get some fat on your bones, eh? Stop worrying, and come with me to our camp. For the present, Outcast Island is your home!"

13

The camp was about half a mile away.

"We built our camp inland because we wanted to be away from the sea," Bác Thong explained to Kien. "We haven't had any really bad storms here yet, but in the monsoon season, the waves will cover Outcast Island."

Kien didn't think much of the camp. Bác Thong's people had built huts out of leaves and branches. These were arranged in a semicircle around a large open cooking pit. Some of the huts were decently constructed, others were falling apart. Apparently each man had built his hut as best he could, without help from anyone.

A group of men were squatting before the cooking pit as Kien and Bác Thong came into camp. One of the men was starting the cooking fire, another piercing several fish on a wooden skewer. A third hacked coconuts open with a wicked-looking knife. All three men looked up as Bác Thong and Kien came into camp, and Kien couldn't be sure if they were friendly.

"Where is the old—my grandfather?" Kien asked, and Bác Thong pointed to a large hut that looked better constructed than the others.

"Until you build your own hut, you are my guests," he said, expansively. "Ah, there is Dr. Phan Tri, talking to your little sister."

Kien hurried over to Mai, who was listening intently to the little doctor.

"He will be very sick for a while," the doctor was saying importantly. "I have given him this medicine, and he will get better, however." Almost grudgingly, he took the bottle of pills from his black bag and counted a few pills into Mai's hand. "Give him four of these each day—one in the morning when you awake, one at noon, one before the evening meal, the last one before you sleep at night."

Mai clutched the precious pills tight as she pressed her hands together and raised them to her forehead, bowing many, many times. Loc, beside her, also bowed his thanks.

Dr. Phan Tri ignored them and turned to Kien. "Ah, yes, the young captain of the *Sea Breeze,*" he said in a cool, slightly mocking voice. "How proud you must be to have brought your family to the safety of Outcast Island. How fortunate for you that your grandfather had charts in his head!"

Kien was puzzled. Dr. Phan Tri somehow did not fit in with Bác Thong and Ahn and the others. He said, "We are lucky to be among friends, on this island."

The doctor snorted with laughter. "Do you call this miserable lump of rock and sand an island? If I had known it was going to be like this, I would never have left! I should not have stepped aboard Bác Thong's miserable, rotting boat when I saw who my companions were going to be. Rough men—many of them thieves or worse in our country. They all do what Bác

153

Thong tells them. They are not my kind of people at all."

"But Bác Thong is kind to us," Kien protested.

"Bác Thong never does anything without a reason. His word is law and everyone obeys. Otherwise . . ." He shook his head. "Here it is every man for himself. When the boat was wrecked, we could have saved the women and weaker men, but no, none of us worked as a team. The longer I live here, the more I am becoming like the others."

Mai and Kien exchanged looks. "Even so, Bác Thong is helping Grandfather!" Loc protested.

"That's because . . ." But before the doctor could say any more, Bác Thong was striding over to them, his round eyes wide and his grin wider still.

"Well, Doctor?" Bác Thong demanded. "How is our patient? Will he be better soon?"

"He'll be all right in a few days," the doctor muttered. He did not meet Bác Thong's eyes.

"Good. Good! Doctor, I'm holding you responsible for the old man's life," Bác Thong said, smiling and smiling. "He's a very valuable old man. Anyone who can sail these waters without a compass or a map . . ." He turned to Mai, Loc, and Kien. "Now, about you —are you hungry? We will soon have food."

"Thank you. Please tell us what to do," Kien spoke automatically, for he was thinking: What had the doctor started to say before Bác Thong came? Is there something Bác Thong wants from us, from Thay Van Chi?

Something was strange. Something was very strange!

He thought about it later while they ate. Mai would not leave the old man, but Kien and Loc ate with

the others around the cooking pit. The food was good
—grilled fish, coconut, and coconut milk mixed with
water. Bác Thong was kindness itself, pressing second
and even third helpings on Kien and Loc.

There had to be some reason for all this kindness,
Kien thought. A group of people who wouldn't cooper-
ate even to save lives would not take in total strangers
and treat them like honored guests for no reason! Kien
hoped that Bác Thong just wanted them off the island
so there wouldn't be extra mouths to feed.

He kept glancing at Bác Thong to see what the
bald man would do next, and he soon found out. After
food came the evening's "entertainment." As soon as
everyone had eaten, Bác Thong ordered several of the
men to clear away the remains of the meal. Coconut
husks, fishbones—everything—was dumped in a pile
some distance from camp. Then Bác Thong clapped his
hands loudly.

"Who will begin the fun?" he shouted.

For a moment, no one moved. Then the big man
who had objected to the newcomers that afternoon got
up.

"I, Ahn, will start," he bellowed.

"Who will stand against Ahn?" Bác Thong demanded. After a short pause, another big man got to his
feet. "Ah, Tranh! All right, boys. Clear away a space!
Give them plenty of room!"

Loc looked at Kien as if to say, What's going on?

Kien shrugged. "We'll soon find out," he muttered.

Quickly, men moved backward, giving Ahn and
Tranh room. The big men faced each other in this
space, and began to circle around. Suddenly, Ahn gave
a terrible shout and rushed at Tranh. The two big man

began to wrestle, kick, and punch.

Loc was frightened. "What are they doing?" he cried.

Bác Thong roared with laughter. "They are providing us with entertainment, little one!" he shouted. "This is Outcast Island, and we have to have something to do in the evenings. There are worse ways to spend a few hours than in watching a good fight."

Kien watched, fascinated, as Ahn and Tranh fought. There seemed to be no rules. Ahn and Tranh tried to hurt each other in every possible way, while the other men cheered—first for Ahn, then for Tranh.

"Remember, the winner gets extra food and does no work tomorrow!" Bác Thong shouted excitedly. "Hit, Ahn! Kick, Tranh!"

Kien had had enough. He shook Loc's shoulder, and the two of them made it back to Bác Thong's big hut. The old man was asleep, but Mai asked, "What is all that awful noise?"

"Entertainment," Kien said shortly. He was deeply troubled now. What kind of people are these? he asked himself. And why, *why* should they want to help us?

The noise outside lasted for most of the night, and Kien pretended to be asleep when Bác Thong returned to the big hut toward dawn. Yet, until Bác Thong fell asleep, Kien lay wide-awake and alert. He wondered what was going to happen when daylight came.

Dawn brought good news. The old man was much better. The terrible fever had broken during the night, and though very weak, Thay Van Chi was himself again. He gathered Loc, Kien, and Mai together, and praised them for all they had done.

"Now tell me about this place," he said. "What is this Outcast Island? Who is Bác Thong?"

"He's a kind man," Mai said, and Loc nodded quickly.

"Yes, he is, Grandfather! He feeds us and he told his doctor to make you well, and he's even going to help repair the *Sea Breeze.*"

Mai shuddered. "He needn't hurry with that on my account," she said. "I don't want even to hear the word 'sea.'"

"All the same, we can't stay here forever," Kien said.

The old man turned to look quickly at Kien. "Why do you say this?"

"It's a small island, for one thing. There haven't been any bad storms here, but I think it would be bad to stay here during the monsoon season. Besides—"

But before Kien could finish, Bác Thong was there in the open doorway of the hut. "Are you men coming to help rebuild your boat?" he demanded, in a friendly way. Then he grinned at Thay Van Chi. "I see you're better, Old One."

"I am grateful," the old man replied. Kien could see how Thay Van Chi looked straight into Bác Thong's round eyes. "It is good of you to help us."

"Nonsense! If we cannot help each other, it would be sad indeed." Bác Thong paused, and then asked very casually, "Do you really know how to get to Malaysia from here?"

"I would need to look at the stars. I would need to discover our latitude. Why do you ask?" Thay Van Chi replied.

"No reason, except that I, too, am a sailor. We could compare notes," Bác Thong said. He turned to Kien and Loc. "Shall we go and see to your boat, men?"

Loc was delighted to be called a man and so trusted

Bác Thong completely. Kien was not so sure. Although he worked with the others, he watched Bác Thong. He noticed the leader of Outcast Island smooth his hand over the sides of the *Sea Breeze* and nod and smile to himself. He listened as Bác Thong ordered that a mast, salvaged from his own wrecked boat, be fitted to the *Sea Breeze* to replace the one the pirates had snapped.

He acts as if the boat were his, Kien thought, and suddenly he realized what he must have known all along. Bác Thong wanted something from them, all right—he wanted the *Sea Breeze*! The *Sea Breeze* was a good, strong boat and would take Bác Thong away from Outcast Island. And he wants Thay Van Chi's knowledge of the sea and stars, he thought to himself. That's why they've been so kind to us! He forced himself to smile at Bác Thong as the bald man came over and put an arm around him.

"Hey, Kien," Bác Thong said, "are you going to sit there and dream? This sail needs repairing. What happened to it, anyway?"

"Pirates shot a machine gun at the sail," Kien answered. To himself, he thought, All right, Uncle, I'll play your game! Using his beggar's whine he added, "Look how those pirates made a sieve of our sail! How can we ever use it again?"

"No need to worry," Bác Thong replied at once. "Together with the mast of my poor old boat, we saved the sails. One of the sails is sure to fit your beautiful strong boat."

"Thank you," Kien said, but in his heart he thought, Now I am sure. But you're never going to get the *Sea Breeze*, Uncle Thong! We'll get the better of you yet!

He had no chance to talk alone to Mai or the old

man that day. Bác Thong seemed always to be around, asking about the old man's health, which was much better. In fact, that evening Thay Van Chi felt strong enough to eat a good meal and even walk a few steps around Bác Thong's big hut.

"That's good, that's good," Bác Thong cried, when he saw how much better the old teacher seemed to be. "Soon we can have that talk about those maps and charts you keep in your head, friend, eh? Eh?" The thought seemed to please him so much that he smiled broadly, showing his protruding teeth.

Kien wondered whether he should tell the others about Bác Thong that night when they were alone. He did not. For one thing, the *Sea Breeze* was not yet sea-worthy. For another, Thay Van Chi was still terribly weak. If we try to get off this island now, he will get sick all over again, Kien thought unhappily. He did not know what to do.

Their third day on Outcast Island was a stormy one. Rain and wind battered the sandy island, and waves roared over the beach, pounding against the coconut palms that lined the shore. Bác Thong frenziedly supervised the mooring of the *Sea Breeze.*

"Do you want this boat harmed after we have worked so hard to get it ready?" he stormed.

Afterward, Bác Thong came back to his hut and spent hours with the old teacher. He demanded that Thay Van Chi draw maps of Malaysia and charts of currents and winds on the dirt floor. Even when the teacher tired, Bác Thong insisted that the old man teach him about steering by the stars and the sun. The kindly, polite Uncle Thong who had greeted them was gone, and Kien realized he had to tell the others what Bác Thong was up to.

When Bác Thong had left the hut, he faced Thay Van Chi squarely. "We may have to leave Outcast Island soon," he said.

"I hope not!" Mai cried. "I've just gotten used to dry land. Besides, Grandfather isn't well yet. I don't want to go back to sea!"

"I like living out here," Loc put in. The few days on the island had done Loc good, and he looked almost like his old, mischievous self. "I don't want to go back either. Storms and raw fish. Ugh!"

But the old man said, "Is it because of the storms, Kien?"

"Yes and no," Kien replied. "When the big storms come, I am sure it's not going to be safe here. But that's not it completely."

"Then it is Bác Thong," the grandfather said, and Kien nodded, relieved that he didn't have to explain to Thay Van Chi. "I suspected as much," the old man breathed.

"What's wrong with Bác Thong?" Mai asked, bewildered. "What has he done?"

"He means to take our boat and leave us here," Kien said flatly.

"I don't believe it! He was so kind to Grandfather and to us! You just don't trust anyone, Kien. That's your trouble."

"Hush," the old man said. "I think Kien is right. That man is too eager to pick my brains. Why should he want to know how to sail to Malaysia unless he wants to take our boat and sail there himself?"

Mai shook her head and covered her ears with her hands. "I don't want to hear about it!" she cried. "We just left the sea, and you've hardly got well, Grandfather!" Her voice rose angrily. "I won't go back to the boat and go to sea again. I won't! I won't!"

"Be quiet," Kien gritted. "Someone might be listening!"

"Let them listen!" Mai shouted. "I am sick of chilled feet that are wet all the time! I don't want to be burned by the sun and half starved and scared silly by storms! I am *sick* of the sea, and I won't go back on the *Sea Breeze*! Ever!"

"Mai!" the old man said sternly, but Mai turned and ran out of Bác Thong's hut into the rain. Thay Van Chi sighed. "It's my fault. She's had to nurse me and she's worried about everything. It's been too much for her." He turned urgently to Kien. "Go after her, Kien!" he commanded. "She mustn't say anything to Bác Thong."

Kien ran into the rain and the storm after Mai. He caught up to her some distance from camp. She was standing in a grove of palm trees, resting her forehead against a tall palm. He thought she was crying, but when he called her name and she turned to him, her eyes were dry.

"Mai," he said. "I'm sorry. It's not good news, is it? But believe me, it's true."

Without a word, she began to walk away from him. He followed, begging her to see sense. Finally she turned to face him. "If we go back to sea, Grandfather will get sick again!" she snapped. "He will die!"

"Not if we get to Malaysia! And, anyway, we can steal some of Dr. Phan Tri's precious pills. He—" Suddenly Kien stopped. "Shh!" he whispered. "Someone's coming!"

"I don't hear—" But Kien grabbed Mai's arm and dragged her behind some tall palm trees. As they hid, they both heard Bác Thong say, "Where are the brats?"

"Last I saw of them, they were in your hut with the Old One," Ahn's voice replied.

"Good. They wouldn't be out in this storm, anyway. How are we doing on the boat, Ahn?"

"It's almost ready, boss. Tomorrow, we'll start loading. Then, by tomorrow evening, we can move out!"

"Move out on *our* boat?" Mai gasped, but Kien hushed her.

"All right. Listen to me, now," Bác Thong went on. "No one must know that we are only taking five people on that boat. Otherwise, we'll have some big fights on our hands."

"Who are we taking, Bác Thong?" Ahn asked respectfully.

"There's you, and there's me. And we have to take Phan Tri. I don't trust him and I don't like him, but he's a doctor and he's useful. Then, we can take Tranh—he's strong. And Tich. He's a handy man with sails and tools. He'll be needed if we have to make repairs on that boat."

"What about the brats and that old man?" Ahn wanted to know.

Bác Thong snorted laughter. "Once the others realize we have left them behind, they'll take out their anger on the Old One and the kids! That'll take care of everything!"

Mai was shivering. "That wicked—that evil man! Kien, you were right!"

"Hush. Listen!" Kien urged. He was shaking, but he forced himself to remain calm and listen closely as Bác Thong and Ahn planned their departure.

"Tomorrow, after our evening's entertainment is over, the five of us will take a walk. Only, we'll never come back," Bác Thong was saying. "The storm will be over by late tonight, and so we'll have clear sailing."

Kien touched Mai's arm, and together they slipped silently away through the rain-drenched palms. Once they were out of earshot, they ran and ran, as though they could escape the evil men of Outcast Island. When they finally stopped running, Mai looked so white and shaken that Kien was worried about her.

"I'm sorry, little sister," he said. "I wish it weren't true!"

"Kien," she said quietly, "if we go to sea, I know some of us will die. I feel it." She put her hands against her chest, and he felt an icy prickle run through his spine as she added, "The sea gave us two chances, Kien. One, we made landfall in Thailand. Now, Outcast Island. It won't give us a third chance to survive."

"If we stay here, we won't live long. You heard what Bác Thong said."

Mai was silent for a long moment, and Kien knew she was trying to be brave. Finally she said, "When must we leave?"

Kien suddenly felt lost and as afraid as Mai. He shook his head.

"I don't know," he said miserably. "I just know we have to leave." He paused. "We'll have to ask your grandfather, Mai."

Mai reached out and took his hand. Wordlessly they trudged back to camp. When they walked into Bác Thong's hut, Loc and the old man were alone. Thay Van Chi looked at Kien, then at Mai and said, "We leave?"

Mai nodded. "We heard them—they're taking the boat and running off with it tomorrow. Grandfather, aren't there any good people left in the world?"

163

The old man did not answer this question, but said firmly, "We must leave tonight, then. I think the storm will lessen and finally die down within an hour or two. The sea will still be rough, but we have been in rougher seas before." He got up, staggered, and rested his hand on Kien's shoulder to support himself.

"We must get some food and water aboard the boat," he whispered urgently. "And if we can, we must take the . . . the pills that made me well . . . from Dr. Phan Tri's black bag!"

"I will get the food," Mai said firmly. Kien looked at her with admiration. Mai didn't waste any time whining, that was sure. Now that it was decided, she was being brave and dependable. "I'll tell the men tonight at supper that you're very hungry, Grandfather," Mai went on. "I'll get some extra coconuts, too. We can collect rainwater in the shells when we're . . . when we're out at sea."

"I'll get the pills," Kien grinned. "It's in my line, shall we say?"

He winked at Mai, who said, with spirit, "Hong always said you were a thief!"

But no one laughed at the little joke. Loc whispered, "What shall I do?" The old man put his arm around his grandson.

"You must be brave and act as if nothing is wrong, my Loc," he said. "You and Kien must eat with those men tonight as though nothing has happened. If they suspect we know what they are up to . . ."

Loc nodded, his eyes huge.

"Don't worry," he said. "I'll pretend everything is fine!" Then his face crumpled and he whispered, "But, Grandfather, I'm afraid."

So are we all, Kien thought. So are we all!

Evening came, and the storm subsided. The stars began to come out, shining white in a moonless sky, and Bác Thong ordered the cooking fires kindled so that they could eat.

When the fish was cooked, Bác Thong gave Mai an extra supply of fish and coconuts without question, but he said, "Tell the old one that tomorrow I am going to ask him more about those maps he carries around in his head!" Mai, without batting an eyelash, nodded.

"I will tell him, Bác Thong," she said. "My grandfather will be only too glad to tell you anything you want to know. After all, you've been so kind to us!"

Kien had to hand it to Mai—she certainly was cool about it! His own palms were sweating at the thought of having to steal Dr. Phan Tri's precious pills. He waited till the meal was over and the evening's entertainment had begun. Then, while two strapping men wrestled and kicked at one another, he nudged Loc and the two of them slipped away.

They hurried to Dr. Phan Tri's hut. While Loc stood guard, Kien hurried inside and felt about in the dark, trying to locate the doctor's black bag. Where does he keep it? Kien wondered.

Finally, he discovered the bag hidden underneath the doctor's palm-leaf bed. Kien snapped open the bag and felt inside for the bottle of pills. Ah, there they were.

"Ssst! Kien! Someone's coming!" Loc hissed. "It's Bác Thong."

Kien shoved the bottle of pills inside his shirt, pushed the bag under the doctor's bed, and raced outside. Too late! As he and Loc began to hurry away from the doctor's hut, Bác Thong's voice demanded, "Where are you two going, eh?"

Kien thought fast, drew a deep breath and managed an impudent laugh. "Well, your entertainment amused Loc so much that he wanted me to show him some wrestling holds. Do you want to see how good he is? Maybe we can wrestle and entertain you all one day!"

Bác Thong began to laugh loudly. "Entertain us? That's a good one." He clapped Kien on the back. "Get on with you. I must pick up Dr. Phan Tri's medicine bag. One of our two fighters got a little hurt . . ."

"That's too bad. Come on, Loc!" Kien was shaking like a leaf as they hurried toward Bác Thong's hut. "Loc, we have to get away—fast! When Dr. Phan Tri opens the bag and realizes the pills are gone . . ."

They burst into the hut at a run. The others were waiting for them. Mai had bundled the food she had collected in a blanket taken from Bác Thong's bed.

"What is it?" she cried. "What's wrong?"

Kien explained, and Thay Van Chi said, "We must go. Now!"

Outside, it was very noisy. The men were still excited from the evening's entertainment and were shouting and stamping and whistling. Under cover of this noise, they hurried through the palm trees toward the shore. The trees, dripping with rain, threw menacing shadows on the ground and terrified them all. They wanted to run, but the old man was still weak and could not move very fast.

They had not reached the shore when Loc suddenly whispered, "Listen!"

Mai's heart leaped into her throat. Borne on the night wind came a loud, angry swell of sound.

"They've found out about us!" Kien groaned. "They'll be coming after us!"

The old man shook himself free of Mai and Kien, who had been helping him along.

"Leave me!" he ordered. "Go without me!"

"We'd never do that!" Mai wailed, and Kien snapped, "How can we get anywhere without you? You know the way to Malaysia!" He tried to think. "Mai, you bring him along as quickly as you can. Loc, help me get the *Sea Breeze* into the water!"

He grabbed the sack of food and propelled the protesting Loc toward the shore. Mai put her arm around her grandfather and together they began to move forward. The old man truly tried to hurry, but his strength gave way before they reached the shore.

"Mai, you must go without me," he panted, but

"Leave me!" Grandfather ordered. "Go without me!"

Mai, without a word, tried to pull him up and onto her back. "Mai . . . don't you hear me?"

Mai could hear *them,* and the sound filled her with terror. Bác Thong and his outcasts were behind her—close behind her. Now Kien was racing toward them across the sand. He helped Mai drag the old man to the *Sea Breeze,* which was waiting on the edge of the water.

"Get him inside! Hurry!" Kien panted.

Loc was already in the *Sea Breeze.* In the starlight Mai could see Loc's eyes, which kept darting to the fringe of palm trees on the shore. "Are they coming?" he wailed. "Will they catch us?"

"Not if we hurry!" And Kien and Mai began to push the *Sea Breeze* into the water.

"Get in the boat!" Kien shouted at Mai. "Hoist the sail. Move!"

As she scrambled into the boat, Kien put his hand into his ragged shorts pocket and pulled out Dr. Phan Tri's bottle of precious pills.

"I don't want them to get wet . . ." he told Mai, who took them and shoved them into her shirt against her skin. She struggled to rig the sail on the *Sea Breeze*'s new mast.

"I can't . . . I can't . . ." she panted.

"Row, then!" Kien shouted. Now the shore was alive with men. Mai could hear Bác Thong shouting for them to stop.

"Row!" Kien cried. He gave the *Sea Breeze* a mighty push into the water, and then struggled over the side of the boat. As Mai grabbed an oar and began to row away from shore, Kien managed to get the sail up.

"Stop them!" Bác Thong yelled, and two men dived into the water. One of them, a small man, began to swim toward the *Sea Breeze* with swift, powerful strokes. The sail unfurled, but there was no wind to carry the *Sea Breeze* to safety. Both Mai and the old man were rowing desperately, but the little man was even more desperate. Now he reached the *Sea Breeze.*

"Stop them!" Bác Thong bellowed from the shore.

More men had leaped into the sea and were swimming toward the *Sea Breeze.* The little man's hands were on the side of the boat, and Mai recognized Dr. Phan Tri.

"You can't take the boat. We need it!" the doctor panted as he began to haul himself in.

Another moment and all those others would reach the *Sea Breeze!* They were lost! Almost without thinking, Mai reached into her shirt and pulled out the bottle of precious pills.

"Here, Doctor . . . I've got something that belongs to you! Want your pills?" she shouted.

Then she threw them high over Phan Tri's head! With a strangled cry, the doctor let go of the boat and began to swim toward the spot where the pills had sunk into the water.

At the same time, wind filled the sails and the *Sea Breeze* began to move away from the land. Quickly and ever more quickly it moved, and behind it, from the shore, rose a long, angry howl of despair.

"Come back!" Bác Thong bellowed. "If I ever catch you . . . Come back!"

No one on the *Sea Breeze* spoke as the boat made for the open water. Then Kien sighed deeply.

"Well," he remarked, "here we are again, heading for Nowhere!"

14

Two days out of Outcast Island, Thay Van Chi's cough returned.

"How stupid I was! Why did I throw those pills at Dr. Phan Tri!" Mai mourned.

"It was the only way to make him let go of the *Sea Breeze*. If the others had caught up to us, we'd never have escaped from Bác Thong," Kien comforted her.

But without the medicine, the old man sickened daily. Each day found him weaker, till he could no longer sail the *Sea Breeze*, even for a few minutes at a time.

By stingily dividing and rationing the few fish and coconuts they had brought with them, they managed to make the food last six days, but at the end of that time there was nothing left, not even a bone or a husk of coconut. Fortunately the monsoons had begun and there was plenty of rainwater. This became their only food.

Where was Malaysia? Kien asked himself over and over as he greedily scanned the horizon. The old man insisted that they were still traveling in the right direction, but could Thay Van Chi be relied upon anymore?

Kien looked at the old teacher anxiously and saw with some surprise that the old man was watching him.

"You are sailing well, Kien," Thay Van Chi said in his weak whisper of a voice. "You will get the *Sea Breeze* to land. I know it."

"When that day comes you'll be right there with us, Uncle," Kien said, trying to make the Old One laugh. But Thay Van Chi closed his eyes and slid into a weak sleep. If only we hadn't had to leave Outcast Island, Kien thought bitterly. That miserable Bác Thong! Kien tried to get angry, angry enough to kill the pain and hunger and worry in him, but the anger didn't work. It only made things worse.

On the seventh day after leaving Outcast Island, Mai herself began to cough. The cough worsened rapidly, till she could hardly breathe for coughing. Loc was by now too weak and listless to care much, but Kien was terrified.

She needs help, he thought. She needs help, now! Otherwise she might . . .

He looked at Thay Van Chi and then at Mai. Help. Where could he find help? He desperately searched the horizon for anything that might give him hope, but there was nothing. No shadow, no sign—nothing.

On the eighth day a squall caught the *Sea Breeze*, spinning the boat around with strong winds and drenching everyone with rain. The next day, the ninth day, the sun came out—ferocious and merciless. Mai was so feverish she was delirious and lay talking nonsense in the bottom of the boat. The old man slept more and more, and Loc sat listlessly by Kien, drowsy from weakness.

Once Loc said, "Kien, do you remember the time I saw you in the forest and called you a Monster Man?"

Kien himself was so weak the thought brought tears to his eyes.

"Yes, little brother," he sighed. "I remember."

"You didn't like us very much, then, Kien. You and Mai were enemies back at the Village," Loc said. "You didn't have many friends."

"No," Kien agreed and hoped Loc would be silent, but the little boy went on.

"You did have a friend once. Remember? The one who gave you the watch. You gave Dao the watch to help us escape." Loc sighed and rested his head against Kien's knee. "It seems a long, long time ago . . ."

Yes, it seemed like a long time ago, Kien thought. He tried to remember how it had felt to be free, uncaring, bound to no one and to no loyalty, and he could not remember. He thought of the promise he had made to himself when Jim went away, the promise that never again would he be hurt by caring for anyone as he had cared for Jim. Then Mai began to cough, and all his other thoughts went away.

I have to get some food for her and the old man or they will die, Kien thought.

Without much hope, he dug around in the wooden sides of the boat until he found an old, rusty hook embedded in the wood. Then, tearing some strands from the blanket Mai had taken from Bác Thong's hut, he fashioned a rude fishline. He had no bait, none at all, and very little hope as he dropped the hook and line over the side of the boat, but the hook would not sink. He looked around the boat for something to weight his line, and then saw something small and bright and colorful protruding from the old man's shirt.

Kien reached for this and saw it was the bag of Vietnamese sand that Thay Van Chi had taken from the beach weeks ago. It was heavy enough to weight the fishing line, but . . .

"You can't use that, Kien!" Loc protested as Kien began to tie the bag of sand to the makeshift fishing line. "Grandfather won't like it!"

"He can't enjoy starving, either," Kien grunted. "Maybe sand from Vietnam will bring us good luck."

Perhaps it was the bright color of the bag that tempted the fish, or perhaps the sand did bring them luck. Within a half hour there was a fish! Kien could hardly believe it as he pulled the fish into the boat. He hastily returned the dripping bag of sand to Thay Van Chi, and then woke the old man and Mai. In silence the fish was divided four ways, and they ate it greedily, gulping bones, fins, and entrails.

"Courtesy of the 'sand of Vietnam,'" Kien said, and when he explained, even the old man smiled.

The "sand of Vietnam" plus the head of the first fish attracted two more fish that day, and the crew of the *Sea Breeze* ate them, too. Now, they felt a little stronger. But Mai's cough was worsening, and Thay Van Chi seemed to be sleeping more and more. Kien did not like it. He knew that people who were very sick often slipped into death in just that way.

Heaven, he prayed within himself, send us some help. We really need it now.

And on the afternoon of the tenth day a ship came.

At first they thought it was just a trick of light, a cloud sweeping low on the horizon. Then Loc, who had regained some of his strength since eating the fish, cried, "Look, Kien! A ship!"

Kien looked up at once, and there it was, painted black and white, with a huge prow that cut through the water like a knife. It really was—

"A ship!" Kien screamed.

Mai sat up and looked around her dazedly.

"Wave your arms! Cry out!" she whimpered, and the old man gasped, "They *must* see us!"

Kien staggered up in the boat and waved his arms wildly. Loc got up and waved too.

"Here we are!" Loc croaked, and Kien shouted, "Come and save us!"

The ship seemed to swing nearer.

Heaven, Kien prayed within himself, send us some help. We really need it now

"It *sees* us!" Loc panted. "Grandfather, Mai, they *see* us!"

The ship was coming nearer still. Kien was filled with such excitement that he couldn't just stand there. With a shout he jumped into the water and began to swim toward the ship.

"I'm here! I'm here!" he gasped, as he made for the ship.

But he had forgotten how weak he was. The spurt of joy could not give him strength, and soon he felt weak all over. Now Kien could see men standing on the deck of the big ship. They were pointing toward him. Any moment now, Kien knew, they would stop.

The ship swept past him in a billowing wash of foaming water that nearly drowned him.

"Don't leave me!" Kien screamed. He began to swim after the ship, but he had no more strength. Water closed over his head. His lungs were bursting. Kicking, he forced himself back to the surface.

One of the men on the deck of the big ship was waving to Kien. He held something in his hand—a round, flat object with a large hole in the middle. A rope was attached to this object, and the man on the deck was making signs to Kien.

"Push your head and shoulders through this opening!" he seemed to say. Kien nodded weakly, and the man on the ship threw the object out into the sea.

It landed near Kien.

"Take hold of that and I'll save you!" the man seemed to be saying.

Desperately, Kien reached for the round object, which was bobbing around some yards away. He pushed himself through the hole in the center of the thing. The man on board nodded in a pleased way and made signs. "Now I am going to pull you on board. You are safe!"

"What about them?" Kien shouted. He jerked his head around, for by now they had passed the *Sea Breeze*. He could see Mai and Loc and the old man, who were all watching him in a bewildered way. "Save them, too!" Kien cried.

The men on the deck all shook their heads. The one who was beginning to haul Kien out of the water shook his head, too. He made a sign to Kien as if to say, "But we are going to save you."

Now Kien understood. The ship was not going to take Loc, Mai, or Thay Van Chi on board. Only he, Kien, would be saved, because he had swum after the boat, and the men on board did not want to see him drown. For a moment, he hung limply from the life saver, staring at the ship. Then he turned back to look at the *Sea Breeze,* already many yards behind him.

If I stay with this ship, Kien thought, I can live!

He wanted to live so much! He wanted to rest, to sleep. Not to worry about food or drink or storms. Mai was sick and the old man was dying. Loc would die soon. They won't blame me if I save myself. I am really not of their family. I don't belong to them.

"I am Kien!" he shouted out loud. "I care for no one! I belong to no one!"

He was being pulled up from the water, foot by foot.

"I want to live!" Kien sobbed. "Don't you understand?"

He turned to look back at the *Sea Breeze* and saw that they were watching him, as if they had heard his cry and understood. And as he looked, Mai waved at him.

Suddenly he saw them all clinging to the mast on the night of the great storm, singing together. He saw Mai feeding the old man that first coconut on Outcast Island, even before she ate anything herself. He felt the gentle touch of the old man's hand.

Without knowing what he did, Kien slid his arms out of the life saver. He felt the water close over his head and kicked himself to the surface. Dazedly he saw that the great ship was moving rapidly away, its deck crowded by watching, pointing men.

"Kien . . . Ki-en!"

The *Sea Breeze* was coming to get him, the old man at the tiller. Kien waited. There were a hundred questions bursting in his mind. Why? he asked himself. Why did I do that?

No one said anything as Kien pulled himself over the side and fell, exhausted, into the bottom of the *Sea Breeze*. As Kien felt again the familiar listing of the boat under him, Loc wailed, "But why didn't they stop for us?"

Mai began to cough. "No one will stop," she whispered. "We are boat people." She looked hard at Kien. "Why didn't you go with them? They would have saved you."

Why? Kien asked himself again, and then he thought, This is the end. It has to be.

15

But there was no easy end.

Pitifully, they continued to live. A fish caught shortly after the big ship passed them by kept them alive for a little while. And rain, falling almost continuously now, furnished them with water. Then there were no more fish, and only rainwater for food and drink. It distended their bellies and made them all so weak they could do nothing but drift and sleep.

Mai was worse, and Kien worried about her more than he worried about the old man. Mai, Kien felt, could still get well, but for the Old One it was only a matter of time. Then, one day, three days after their sighting of the big ship, Thay Van Chi woke from one of his long sleeps and appeared much stronger and very clear in his mind.

"Do you know our position?" he asked Kien.

Kien shook his head. "I've given up on a position," he admitted. "I don't know where we are. We could have sailed in a complete circle and I wouldn't know it." He stopped and looked hard at Thay Van Chi and added happily, "But you are better! Perhaps the crisis has passed and you can guide us again."

"It is said that before the end the lamp burns strongest," the old man said quietly. "It is so for me. I am dying, Kien."

"Don't talk like that!" Kien cried angrily. "What good does it do?"

"The truth must be faced," the old man said calmly. "I am sorry, for you will have to bear the burden, Kien. You are the oldest of this family."

"I am not—" Kien began.

But Thay Van Chi interrupted him to say, "You are also the strongest. You will survive the longest. It will be hardest for you."

"I don't want to listen to you," Kien said savagely, but the old man put his hand into his shirt and drew out the little colorful bag of Vietnamese sand.

"This is yours now," he said. "I give it to you."

"I don't want it. It has nothing to do with me. What good will it do me?"

"If you survive, you must keep my promise to return to Vietnam someday. It is our country, our beloved country, and though you may roam the earth, Kien, you must not forget it. You must someday return to Vietnam and say that Thay Van Chi kept his word."

Kien wanted to cry with frustration. The old man was looking at him. "You must carry out my dying wish," he said sternly.

"Old man," Kien said loudly, "I am not bound to you in any way. You are not my family. I belong to no one! I am here with you because all of us wished to escape from Guyen Thi Lam. Your dying wish does not concern me!"

"I have watched you change," Thay Van Chi said to Kien. "At first you were a beggar child who knew only how to survive through his wits, who would hurt and steal and lie to survive. Then that beggar child grew to care for the people of our Village. And when danger came to the Village, you gave up a precious keepsake to buy our safety." The old man closed his eyes, but his voice was strong. "I saw you risk your life to save Loc from the shark, and I have seen you weep when Mai

Kien saw that the wise old eyes
had become fixed and glazed

coughs. Why would you have returned to us from that big ship, which would have saved you alone, if you did not care for any of us?"

Kien could say nothing. "I wish I had gone with them!" he finally cried, defiant. "I wish I had left you to die!"

"But you could not. Mai and Loc are your family, now," the old man said. Gently he added, "Kien, none of us choose to be born into a family. Heaven wills that. Nor do we choose those we come to love."

Kien bowed his head and thought, It's true. After Jim, I never cared for anyone. I never wanted to care whether you lived or died, old man. I never meant this to happen.

"As my oldest grandson, you must promise to carry out my dying wish," the old man whispered. "Take care of Loc and Mai. You are the strongest."

Kien whispered back, "I will do what you ask."

The old man said nothing. Kien saw that the wise old eyes had become fixed and glazed. Thay Van Chi was dead.

As if the old teacher could still hear him, Kien went on, "I will carry out your promise someday. It is true. I have come to love you, my grandfather. I have come to love you all."

Only then did he begin to weep.

16

They buried the old teacher at dawn, singing together the folksong they had sung on the night of the great storm. Loc cried desperately, but Mai was quite calm.

"Look how peaceful he is and how happy," she comforted Loc. "Nothing will hurt him anymore." To herself she added, "And soon we will be with him and everything will be all right."

Kien heard her, and fear gripped tightly around his heart. He remembered what Mai had said to him on Outcast Island, that the sea would not give them another chance. He glared at the sea.

"You will save Mai and Loc," he whispered fiercely. "I demand you save Mai and Loc!"

He watched the horizon all that day, praying, demanding, a ship, a line, or a smudge on the horizon that might mean landfall. The boat was so quiet, now that the old man was gone. Kien found himself missing Thay Van Chi terribly. Many times he would catch himself glancing at the spot where Thay Van Chi had sat, only to find it empty. Whenever this happened, he took the bright bag of sand out from his shirt and held it very tightly in his hand.

Another day came, and then another. There was no fish, no rain. They had stopped trying to steer or even sail, and the boat went where the winds and currents took it. When, on the third day, a mass of clouds formed on the horizon Kien was almost grateful that a storm would bring them rain, even though he knew that after every storm, not only they but the *Sea Breeze* too would get weaker. Lately he had felt a difference in the boat, something he could sense more than he could explain. Kien knew that the hull of the good old boat was tiring after such a long time in the water. One of these days the *Sea Breeze* would break apart. And then . . .

Kien did not like to think of death, but he hoped it would come painlessly. When he heard Mai coughing and coughing, he sometimes wished death would come quickly.

He tried to prepare Loc and Mai for the storm that was to come. Mai was a little out of her head with fever and smiled when Kien told her of the coming squall.

"I feel Grandfather is here in the boat," she murmured.

Kien felt a shiver creep up his spine. "Mai," he said, as gently as he could, "the old man is dead."

"I know that. I don't mean it that way. But I dreamed about him a few minutes ago, and he was smiling at us and said that everything would be over soon. Doesn't that mean that this storm will be the end of us? And that we will be with him . . . at peace?"

Kien said nothing. He dipped his hands into the cool sea and began to wash down Mai's hot forehead and arms. She whispered, "Kien, maybe it's better this way. No one wants us. We have no home, no country, nothing. We have nothing at all."

"Stop feeling sorry for yourself!" Kien said roughly, but inside he was crying. He cooled Mai down as best he could and then went over to Loc. Loc was very weak and drowsy and only half opened his eyes as Kien sat beside him. "You must wake up, little brother," Kien told Loc. "A storm is coming."

"A bad storm?" Loc asked, and Kien shook his head.

He caught himself praying that the storm be very, very bad—bad enough to finish this, once and for all.

He could not bear the thought of Mai and Loc dying before his eyes. It would be easier, better, to go all together.

Aboard the freighter *Camelot,* Frank Hardman was taking a morning stroll. He always liked to be up and on deck right after a storm. A storm always seemed to clear the heavy tropical air and sweep the seas clean.

"Good morning, Frank!" It was the skipper of the *Camelot,* Captain Dubois. "It looks very peaceful this morning," he went on.

"It wasn't very peaceful last night, sir." Frank Hardman had been Dubois's first officer for many years, and they had gone through many storms together. "A regular storm that was."

"So it was. Pity all the smaller craft that—Frank, do you see something out there? To starboard."

The first officer stared. "No, I don't. Yes, I do! It looks like some kind of boat."

The skipper had binoculars hanging around his neck. He lifted them to his eyes and whistled. "There seem to be people on board."

"*Here?* In the middle of the South China Sea? Where do you think they came from, Skipper? Borneo?"

"Vietnam, I think. Boat people. Here, have a look."

Frank Hardman took the binoculars and looked long and hard. He saw the small fishing boat with the bare mast. A tangle of sail lay at the bottom of the boat. And in the boat . . .

"Children," he breathed. "My God. Children! Why?"

"So many of them leave Vietnam," Dubois mused. "Many are drowned. Some starve. Others are killed by pirates. The ones who survive all that usually end up in refugee camps, unless they can find sponsors or countries willing to take them in. I wonder why, too!"

Frank Hardman turned to his skipper. "Are we going to stand around philosophizing or are we going to pick those kids up?" he demanded.

The captain paused for a moment, then said, "Get them aboard, Frank. Lord knows how that miserable little boat of theirs survived last night's storm! And they . . . they're lying very still too. Let's hope we aren't too late!"

They had been on the sea forever. They had drifted on water forever. In between sleep and waking, Kien remembered how he had tied Loc and Mai and himself to the mast last night, how he had clung to them, talked to them, sung to them, begged them to stay alive for one more night, one more day.

For what? Kien wondered wearily.

There was a sound somewhere near him. He opened his eyes—and saw the ship.

He did not believe it was really there. "You are only a dream," he told the ship. "Go away!"

But the ship stayed where it was. And then there came men in uniforms who lifted Mai and Loc and Kien himself out of the *Sea Breeze*. Loc woke up as a sailor's arms lifted him, and he began to scream for his grandfather.

"It's all right, little brother," Kien told him. "A ship came, that's all."

He could not believe it. The miracle had happened. And everything was moving so quickly, Kien could make no sense out of it. On the deck of the strange ship, there was confusion. There were tall men there, who seemed very concerned and upset when Mai was brought on board and wrapped in several blankets. One of the tall men—perhaps a doctor?—took Mai's pulse, and issued orders in a language that Kien did not exactly know, but which he recognized.

"American," he said aloud, and from the long-ago past when he had been Jim's friend, he said, "You . . . friend? Okay?"

"Do you speak English?" one of the men on deck asked, but Kien could only shake his head.

"Take care of my brother and sister," he whispered brokenly in Vietnamese. "They are sick."

Now yet another of these strange men was kneeling in front of Loc. "Don't worry about anything," this man said in fairly good Vietnamese. "Everything is all right, now."

"Mai?" Kien twisted his head to look. They were giving Mai an injection. Loc did not know what they were doing to his sister and began to howl.

"Don't worry!" Kien shouted to Loc. "It's all right!"

"The doctor is going to take your sister down to a cabin and examine her," the man in front of Kien said. "Here is milk. Drink it."

Kien saw that Loc was being given milk, too, and drank. He had never tasted anything so sweet or so good as this milk, and he had tears in his eyes when he finished. He was surprised that the man before him was also crying.

"Dear God," the man said, in English, and then in Vietnamese he added, "How long have you been at sea?"

"Days . . . weeks . . . years . . . I don't know. We had the . . . we had our grandfather with us until some days ago. But he died."

He would have said more, but his legs buckled under him, and it seemed as if the world was spinning round and round. The man who had been talking to Kien now lifted him in his arms, and another big sailor picked Loc up, soothing him as gently as a mother. Loc and Kien were taken below to a small room where there were four beds—two on the floor, two suspended from the wall.

Mai was lying in one of the beds. The doctor was still with her, and when Kien looked a passionate question, the man nodded and smiled. "She will be all right," he said.

He had spoken in English, but Kien understood even before the words were translated. "You will all be all right," the one who could speak Vietnamese said. "Don't worry about anything. By heaven, I'll sponsor you myself."

Kien was lifted into one of the top bunks. He

watched as Loc was gently tucked into the bunk next to Mai, and then he slowly sank into the soft, clean sheets. More milk was given to him.

"There will be more when your stomach can hold it," his new friend said. "Sleep now, and don't worry. It's over."

But there was something left for Kien to do.

After the men had left the room, Kien put his hand into his shirt and pulled out the small bright bag of Vietnamese sand. He took it in his two hands and pressed the bag against his forehead.

"My grandfather," he whispered, "I am going to keep my promise. My grandfather, Mai and Loc and I are together and safe."

And suddenly it seemed to Kien as if the old man knew and was there, smiling at him, loving, approving everything he did. Gently the wise old hands seemed to be smoothing Kien's hair, lifting the sheets to cover him. Now, Kien knew, he could rest.

Somewhere, out on the wide sea, her work done, the *Sea Breeze* was finishing her voyage alone.

Somewhere, out on the wide sea, her work done, the Sea Breeze was finishing her voyage alone

VIETNAMESE AND THAI WORDS

VIETNAMESE:

Bác	Uncle—a term of respect for an older man
Cho	Wait
Coi chung	Be careful
Thay	Teacher. Also used as part of a name, e.g., Teacher Van Chi
Thoi-dii	Stop . . . that's enough
Toi chong mat	I am dizzy
Toi ten la Kien	My name is Kien

THAI:

Dii mak	Very good
Iut	Stop
Pai ban	Go home

ABOUT THE AUTHOR

MAUREEN CRANE WARTSKI was born in Ashiya, Japan, and lived there until she was seventeen. She attended the University of Redlands in California and Sophia University in Tokyo.

A writer since she sold her first story at age fourteen, she often writes about the many countries she has visited, especially the countries of Southeast Asia. She has also taught English and history overseas, and in Sharon, Massachusetts, where she lives with her husband, Mike, and their sons Bert and Mark.